FLiRT

Write Here, Right Now

By Nicole Clarke

GROSSET & DUNLAP
Published by the Penguin Group
Penguin Group (USA) Inc., 375 Hudson Street,
New York, New York 10014, U.S.A.
Penguin Group (Canada), 90 Eglinton Avenue East,
Suite 700, Toronto, Ontario, Canada M4P 2Y3
(a division of Pearson Penguin Canada Inc.)
Penguin Books Ltd, 80 Strand, London WC2R 0RL, England
Penguin Ireland, 25 St Stephen's Green, Dublin 2, Ireland
(a division of Penguin Books Ltd)
Penguin Group (Australia), 250 Camberwell Road,
Camberwell, Victoria 3124, Australia
(a division of Pearson Australia Group Pty Ltd)
Penguin Books India Pvt Ltd, 11 Community
Centre, Panchsheel Park, New Delhi - 110 017, India
Penguin Group (NZ), Cnr Airborne and Rosedale Roads,
Albany, Auckland 1310, New Zealand
(a division of Pearson New Zealand Ltd)
Penguin Books (South Africa) (Pty) Ltd, 24 Sturdee
Avenue, Rosebank, Johannesburg 2196, South Africa

Penguin Books Ltd, Registered Offices:
80 Strand, London WC2R 0RL, England

Cover and interior design by Michelle Martinez Design, Inc.
Illustrations by Marilena Perilli

Library of Congress Cataloging-in-Publication Data

Clarke, Nicole.
  Write here, right now / by Nicole Clarke.
    p. cm. — (Flirt ; 1)
  Summary: Having left her Berkeley, California, home for an eight-week summer internship at a New York City fashion magazine, Mel tries to cope with her new roommates and with city life as she follows her dream of becoming a writer.
  ISBN 0-448-44263-9 (pbk.)
  [1. Internship programs—Fiction. 2. Authorship—Fiction. 3. Fashion—Fiction. 4. Self-confidence—Fiction. 5. New York (N.Y.)—Fiction.] I. Title. II. Series.
  PZ7.C55433Wri 2006
  [Fic]—dc22

2005029084

10 9 8 7 6 5 4 3 2 1

FLiRT

Write Here, Right Now

By Nicole Clarke

Grosset & Dunlap

chapter one

"Champagne for the lady?"

Melanie Henderson didn't even bother to look up because—*hello?*—the flight attendant must have been talking to someone other than her underage self.

Besides, Mel was too immersed in her journal to gaze enviously at the other passengers accepting their glasses of bubbly. Usually on plane rides, Mel was so cramped that she couldn't get her tray table down over her hunched-up knees, much less find a comfortable writing angle. But today, everything was different! For the first time in Mel's life (and limited travel history), she'd been bumped up to first class, where she could stretch out her long legs, sprawl comfortably in her roomy seat, and even prop her so-new-it-crackled journal on a superwide arm rest and scribble to her heart's content. Yup. She was going to fly from San Francisco to New York City in style, bay-bee!

Just without champagne.

"Excuse me? Miss? Did you hear me?"

Mel finally looked up, her blue-gray eyes wide, and stifled a gasp.

Turned out the flight attendant *was* talking to Mel. "Oh . . ." Mel said. She scanned the small cabin quickly, wondering if anyone was shooting her an accusatory glare, but all the other well-heeled passengers seemed immersed in their own little worlds. And their own glasses of champagne.

"Why not?" Mel said, sweeping up a flute with her long, delicate fingers as if it were the most normal thing in the world. "It's a long flight east, isn't it? Cheers!"

"Cheers," the attendant replied with a smile. "Now please let me know if you need anything else. I'll be coming around with a menu as soon as wheels are up."

"Great!" Mel said. She'd already taken a big slug of the bubbly and it had given her an instant fizzy feeling. Back home in Berkeley, the most she ever got to drink was the occasional plastic cup of stinky beer during a keg party. And that stuff was so gross, she rarely touched it. But champagne was new! And champagne—Mel instantly decided—she liked.

"Heading home?" said a rumbly voice.

Mel jumped again. This time, the voice came from the man sitting in the window seat next to her.

"Leaving home, actually," Mel said, taking another sip (okay, slurp) of champagne. Over the rim of her glass, she checked the guy out. He looked like he was in his late twenties, or maybe even his early thirties. But other than that, he was an undisputed hottie. His dark blond hair did that same wavy-curly leap off his forehead as Patrick Dempsey's. Come to think of it, his jaw was chiseled just like Patrick's, too.

So sue me, Mel thought. *I have a thing for older guys. Not that anything has ever come of it beyond a few dates with high school seniors.*

Mel was about to sigh, when another voice reminded her: *But that could all change now! Your whole life is gonna change. You're about to spend the summer in New York City working at a world-famous magazine. Why shouldn't your dating pool get better, too?*

The realization made Mel so giddy that she had the urge to flip open her journal and scribble down her latest "thought."

That was pretty much what her journal had always been for her: a somewhat incredulous list of her coups and triumphs, from winning high school writing awards to being asked to model in an ad for Nuts 'n Berries, the coolest Birkenstock and peasant skirt parlor in Berkeley.

Of course, you couldn't commit coups or triumphs with your nose buried in a notebook so—for the moment—Mel left her journal closed.

"I'm spending the summer in Manhattan," she told the hottie. "What? Did you think I was a New Yorker? I'm flattered!"

66 *Clearly, you're a model.* **99**

"Well, you're drinking champagne," Hottie said, nodding at Mel's almost-empty flute, "and you're probably taller than me by a good three inches. Clearly, you're a model."

Mel almost spewed her last swallow of bubbly all over Hottie's obviously expensive shirt.

"I work in the fashion industry," Hottie added with a dry laugh.

Mel laughed along with him as the crisply coiffed flight attendant made her way up the aisle, collecting their champagne glasses for takeoff.

"Well, that's something we have in common," Mel said, raising her seat back to the full and upright position. "At least for the next eight weeks."

"If you're not modeling, what *are* you doing?" Hottie wondered. Was Mel imagining it or were the guy's green eyes going all winky and flirty on her?

"I'm writing," Mel declared, feeling her cheeks go even pinker.

After a few minutes, the move-about-the-cabin chime pinged through the plane. Almost instantly, the flight attendant appeared at Mel's elbow, two more flutes of champagne at the ready. Hottie reached across Mel, took both the glasses and handed one to her.

"Cheers," he said.

"Cheers," Mel replied with a wide smile.

Clink!

ⓖ   ⓖ   ⓖ   ⓖ

"Sho here's the thing," Mel slurred, stretching her legs out and angling her seat back. She and Hottie, who had instructed her to call him Quinn, were now several hours into the flight—and their conversation.

"This internship thing?" Mel said. "It's just the beginning. A shtepping shtone, you could shay. That is, if I could shay it!" She giggled loudly.

"To something more . . . sherious," Mel said with another giggle. She'd stopped drinking after three glasses of champagne. Or was it four? But her nose still felt a little ticklish and her head felt very heavy on her slender neck.

"Oh, you sound *really* serious," Quinn teased.

"No, no, no," Mel drawled. "You don't undershtand. I mean, I know *Flirt* is a major player. It's huge! But it's also about *fashion*. Lipstick and leg warmers are cool and all, but I really see myself, y'know, writing about Sudanese refugees, or the women's movement in Afghanistan. I want to write a biography of Debbie Stoller or a book of essays about improving education. I want to write those stories in *The New Yorker* that everybody talks about for months!"

"Oh," Quinn said drily. "Is *that* all? I can't wait to hear how it goes."

" This internship thing? It's just the beginning. A shtepping shtone, you could shay. "

"Quinnnnn," Mel cooed. "Is this your way of saying you want to keep in touch?" Was he going to ask for her number now?

"Oh, I have a feeling we'll run into each other again," Quinn said with a smug smile.

Mel cringed.

Okay, she thought, feeling her giddiness deflate suddenly. *I think that was a big, fat rejection.*

"Melanie," Quinn explained quietly. "I'm old enough to be your, well, if not your father, definitely your uncle. But it's been fun talking to you. Very enlightening, indeed."

"You too," Mel muttered, feeling her cheeks go red.

"Now, if you'll excuse me," Quinn said, whipping a royal blue eye mask out of his seat pocket, "I think I'm going to take a catnap for the last bit of the flight. Wake me when we hit LaGuardia!"

Within seconds, he was snoozing.

Which meant Mel had an entire hour of flight time left to squirm. Maybe another glass of champagne would help?

Mel reached for the flight attendant call button. In minutes, she had another flute in hand. Since she had nobody to toast with, she reached across the armrest to Quinn's tray table, which held a half-full glass of water.

Clink!

Okay, Mel thought over an hour later, *you know you've had too much to drink when the spinning of a baggage carousel makes you dizzy!*

She was standing, shaky-legged, in LaGuardia airport's baggage claim, scrubbing at her makeup-free eyes as she tried to focus on the luggage circling before her. It had been fifteen minutes and her bag was still eluding her.

"Great," Mel muttered to herself. "My luggage is lost. Not only am I going to be late to my orientation lunch at *Flirt*, but I'm also going to arrive without a change of clothes, a pair of non-flip-flopping shoes, even a *toothbrush* to my name."

"Excuse me? Miss Henderson?"

Feeling a gentle tap on her shoulder, Melanie peeked behind her. She was looking into the jowly face of a man in a black suit. In his pudgy hands was a sign that said *M. Henderson—Flirt.*

"M. Henderson!" Mel exclaimed with relief. "That's me!"

"I had a feeling," the man said, giving her an appraising look. "I'm Jared Arno. I've been standing here for ten minutes. You didn't see me? Or my enormous sign?"

"I guess the, er, flight made me a little woozy." Mel cringed.

"Not a problem," the man said briskly. "With me driving, we'll get you to the Hudson-Bennett building on time. Now, where's your bag?"

"See, that's the problem," Mel shrugged, pulling nervously at a tendril of hair that had fallen out of her messy bun. "I don't seem to see it . . ."

"What's it look like?" Jared said quickly.

"Um, it's a black duffel?" Mel said. "With turquoise handles and an orange luggage tag."

Jared, who was even taller than Mel, peered over the throng crowding the carousel, then plunged into it. Within three minutes, he'd emerged with Mel's bulging, packed-at-the-last-minute duffel.

"But how did you—?" Mel stuttered. "Where was—? I didn't see—?"

"The first thing you've gotta learn about the magazine business," Jared said to Mel, "is sometimes there's no time to ask questions. You just got to go with things and move on."

Jared swung her heavy duffel over his shoulder and began to lead her outside. To a limo. A glossy, black car stretched out to ridiculous lengths.

"We're riding in *that*?" Mel gaped.

"What? You were expecting a Schwinn?"

Melanie hesitated for a moment before the car's back door. Suddenly the bubbly, champagney feeling in her stomach morphed into nervous flutters. All the ridiculous, champagne-induced bravado she'd had on the plane began to melt away.

This is the big leagues, Mel realized, perhaps for the first time since being awarded this internship several months earlier.

She took a deep breath and reached for the car door.

"Oh, no you don't!" Jared called. He swept over and grabbed the handle before Mel could get to it. Then he opened the door with a great flourish.

Mel balked at Jared.

"Dude," she said. "Back in Berkeley? We open our own car doors. Letting folks wait on you hand and foot isn't exactly progressive, y'know."

"Well, Dorothy," Jared said with a gleam in his eyes, "you're not in Berkeley anymore."

He bowed deeply and waved Mel into the car. Which made her burst out laughing.

Mel sank into the back-facing seat and settled into the car's plushness. As a vegetarian, she didn't approve of the leather seats, but she had no argument with the huge, comfy arm rest nested between the two seats, the TV screen hovering over her head, or the miles of legroom for her to stretch out in.

As Jared got behind the wheel and started driving, Mel foraged in the bar and pulled out a bottle of Perrier. She took a big swig to wash some of the champagne fuzz out of her mouth. This time, the bubbles served to wake her up a little.

"Hey, Jared," she called over her shoulder.

"Yeah?" Jared replied.

"We're not gonna be met at the Hudson-Bennett building by paparazzi, are we?" Mel quipped. "You know, pulling up in this starlet car?"

"Please," Jared said, zipping the limo onto a highway. "In this town, nobody even notices a 'starlet car.' You *are* going to be met by Josephine Bishop, though. So get ready."

"What do you mean?" Mel said, thoroughly surprised. "She's the editor-in-chief of a fashion magazine, not Donald Trump."

"Your point being . . . ?" Jared asked, glancing back at Mel with raised eyebrows.

"I don't know," Mel said. "I guess I pictured Josephine Bishop being all young and hip. I thought we'd have editorial meetings in her funky office, sitting on the floor with our shoes off, eating Skittles. That she'd be kind of like a big sister to all of us."

"Whoa," Jared said. "You really don't know Ms. Bishop."

" I pictured Josephine Bishop being all young and hip. I thought we'd have editorial meetings in her funky office, sitting on the floor with our shoes off, eating Skittles. "

"Oh," Mel quavered. "Okay, I get it. You're saying she's not exactly the Skittles-eating type."

"Hmm, I gotta admit, it's hard to picture Ms. Bishop eating anything." Jared shrugged as he steered the limo into a tunnel. "She's kinda like a good diamond, see? Flawless. And so is her magazine. From what I've heard, that's because she keeps her staff hopping."

"Oh," Mel said again. She gazed out the limo's tinted window at the dingy tunnel walls and processed this new information.

When the limo emerged from the tunnel, Mel gasped. All she could see through the car window was an endless swath of tall buildings, packed together like sardines and as awe-inspiring as the deep canyons Mel liked to hike back home.

A moment later, the car plunged right into the pack of buildings. The sunlight grew dimmer as the limo was engulfed in New York's beautiful chaos. Mel stared, open-mouthed, at stately, elegant apartment buildings, giant department stores, subway stops, newsstands filled with fluttering periodicals, and burly hot-dog vendors hawking their wares in dirty aprons and backward baseball caps.

Almost as fascinating were the New Yorkers themselves. They almost looked like a different breed of people than the sun-kissed, laid-back Californians Mel knew back home. Professional types in suits and high heels stalked the sidewalks with haughty confidence. Milling among them were artsy kids in ripped-up, DIY outfits, ladies-who-lunch wearing prim designer duds, and student types in jeans, tank tops, and iPod earbuds.

Mel loved New York at first sight. She could have driven around for an hour, soaking up her first impressions of the city, but after only a few minutes of gawking, Jared pulled up to a curb.

Mel practically laid down on the car seat to peer out of the limo's window and take in her first eyeful of the Hudson-Bennett building.

If Ms. Bishop was intimidating, this building was like the wizard's castle in Oz—a giant art-deco pillar of gray stone, fronted by three giant glass-and-brass doors, over which loomed the etched words THE HUDSON-BENNETT COMPANY EST. 1923.

> **If Ms. Bishop was intimidating, this building was like the wizard's castle in Oz.**

"Whoa," Mel breathed.

The limo door flew open, and a young woman with porcelain skin, a glossy red ponytail, and poochy, terra-cotta-glossed lips thrust her head into the backseat. She introduced herself by saying crisply, "You're late! Come with me."

Mel grabbed her big orange backpack and plunged out of the car. She almost had to run to keep up, even though the redheaded woman was about five feet tall and wearing superhigh heels.

"I'm Delia," she called over her shoulder, "Josephine

Bishop's personal assistant. We're going straight to the orientation lunch in the cafeteria. It would have been much easier had you arrived in New York yesterday, like the other five interns. But since you insisted on flying out today, you'll just have to jump right in."

Mel gulped. She supposed it wouldn't help to tell Delia that she'd tried to get an earlier flight. But—given that Mel had sort of forgotten to make her reservation until two weeks ago—today's early-morning trip had been the only option left.

As she and Delia rushed into the lobby of the Hudson-Bennett building, Mel felt the same swoop in her belly that she'd experienced on the plane.

The lobby felt more like a train station, one of those grand old terminals with flying buttresses. There was a looming, faraway ceiling, marble tile floors, a sleek, chrome reception desk, and a bank of busy elevators lining the back wall.

It was the grandest place Mel had ever seen.

And the *flip-flop-flip* of Mel's shoes definitely didn't sound right on the marble tile. Delia's sexy *click-click-click* was much more appropriate.

Which made Mel wonder if she was ready after all.

Delia pulled a laminated badge out of a pocket in her skinny skirt as she whisked past a lanky security guard at the front desk.

"She's with me, Paulie," she said brusquely. "And

late for orientation. I promise I'll bring her down for mug shots and fingerprints after lunch."

"Really?" Mel gasped. "Fingerprints?"

Delia didn't bother to answer. She was too busy running toward an open elevator.

"Hold the door, please!" she called to a trio of women inside. Like Delia, each of these women was decked out in spiky-heeled pumps, superskinny skirts, and tops whose fabric hung in silky, creamy folds.

"People call them Hudson-Bennettons," Mel remembered Quinn telling her on the plane. *"Everybody in New York knows about the Hudson-Bennettons."*

Delia ushered Mel into the elevator, pushed the PH button, and without missing a beat, scoffed, "They don't really take your fingerprints. Flirt isn't *really* like jail. Except those deadline days when we all pull all-nighters."

"Sounds . . . fun," Mel said.

Delia looked at her blankly, then handed her the fat folder she'd been carrying. It was emblazoned with the funky *Flirt* logo.

"In there," Delia explained, "you've got your company policies, a schedule of events that interns are expected to attend—such as the big RunCatchKiss fashion show next week—a list of responsibilities, the names and duties of staffers, exemplary articles you should study, and myriad other chapters in the *Flirt* bible. If I were you, I'd study up. It won't look good to waste editors' time with questions that are answered in bold print in your packet."

Mel took a deep breath.

The folder was the size of a dictionary. Mel staggered under its weight.

Okay, why do I have the feeling, she thought, *that college is gonna be a breeze after my summer at* Flirt?

Suddenly, the elevator doors swept open.

And once again, Mel had to stifle a gasp.

When Delia had mentioned the cafeteria, Mel had pictured your usual linoleum-tile-plastic-tray-and-steam-table affair.

The Hudson-Bennett caf? Picture a cross between a New York City loft and something out of *Star Wars.* The food stations were made of brushed steel and blue-tinted Lucite. Sleek silver banquettes, kidney-shaped tables, and aerodynamic beech-wood chairs lined the dining room. The light fixtures seemed to explode like comets. The space was pumping with house music that was just the right decibel for easy chat.

Mel had drank way more than she'd eaten that morning. Now that her loopiness had ebbed away (to be replaced by a sort of post-drunk haze) she was ravenous. She gazed longingly at the pasta and omelette station, the panini press, and the soup tureens, all of which were curiously neglected by the Hudson-Bennettons. Instead, everybody was crowded around the salad bar, nudging one another out of the way to dive for arugula and snow peas. It all looked appetizing to Mel, but Delia was leading her in the opposite direction.

"The catering division set up a lunch for you in the meeting area," she said. She led Mel down a long, undulating aisle that skimmed between the banquettes and a gauntlet of tables. Mel watched coiffed heads swivel automatically as they passed.

"Is it just me?" Mel murmured, "or do you think we're being watched?"

"It's not just you," Delia snapped, giving Mel's flip-flops a withering glance. "They call this the catwalk."

For the first time since getting off the plane, it occurred to Mel what she must look like. Her earthy, wash-and-wear look fit like a glove in Cali. But at *Flirt*?

Mel had a feeling it wasn't gonna fly.

And she got confirmation of that the moment she and Delia stepped through a shimmery blue partition into a small dining area. A long, narrow table was full of people, but only one of them drew—no, *commanded*—Mel's full attention. It was a woman sitting at the table's head. Her back was ramrod straight and her face was a portrait of chilly composure, even in profile.

That has *to be Josephine Bishop*, Mel thought.

Bishop's straight hair was cut into a perfect, shoulder-skimming dark bob with long bangs that just hit her perfectly arched eyebrows. Her tall, slender self was poured into an elegant ivory pantsuit. She wore pearls around her neck, in her earlobes, and clacking like charms around her wrist.

She glanced over as Mel entered the room and rose from her chair in one graceful motion. When she strode over to Mel, her heels clacked authoritatively.

Bishop didn't welcome Mel.

She didn't say hello or introduce herself.

She just looked Mel up and down like a drill sergeant inspecting a soldier. Her bright blue eyes skimmed from Mel's exposed and unpainted toenails to the uneven hem of her peasant skirt to her slouchy layered tanks to her disheveled topknot. Then Bishop's lip curled upward until it reached full-on sneer status.

Oh, God, Mel thought. *She hates me on sight!*

But Bishop still didn't say anything. She just nodded again and returned to her seat.

"Now we may begin," she said. "Melanie, please help yourself to some lunch . . ."

Ms. Bishop pointed a graceful finger at a banquette against the wall.

". . . and take your seat as quickly as possible."

As Mel hurried to the banquette, she had a brief moment to scan the other faces in the room. She saw a host of adults who must have been editor/writer/administrator types. Their looks seemed to fall into two categories. Half of them were frazzled beyond belief, complete with gray under-eye circles, frizzed-out hair, and all-black ensembles that no doubt hid a world of coffee stains and other sins. The other half were coiffed with Bishop-style sharpness.

Against this landscape of elders, five girls—*the five other interns,* Mel realized with a quick inhale—stood out. Not only were they young and fresh-faced, they were gorgeous, arrayed in one multiculti row. Mel quickly assessed. There was an Asian girl wearing a black vinyl minidress tripped in orange and pink sporty stripes, a prim blonde who reminded Mel of Princess Diana, a voluptuous babe with giant brown eyes and a scarf wrapped chicly around her wavy black hair, and finally, a pair of brown-haired girls who were leaning toward each other and eyeing Mel with gossip-hungry eyes. They looked as if they were on the cusp of whispering to each other.

I just hope they'll say something sympathetic, Mel thought, feeling squirmy and self-conscious as she turned to focus on the banquette's munchies.

Her face fell when she found none of the pasta, soups, or omelettes she'd spied in the cafeteria. Here, there were only bowls of small salads (the dressing on the side) and some tiny sandwiches cut into dainty, crustless triangles.

Mel helped herself to three of them, a salad, and a Diet Coke (since no regular ones were offered). Then she hurried to the table.

"Editors, please introduce yourselves," Ms. Bishop said the moment Mel sat down.

One by one, the adults began to speak.

"I'm Julia Danes," said the first woman. "I work in Letters to the Editor, which is much more crucial to a magazine's core than many people would have you know . . ."

Mel tried to listen, really she did. But she was also trying to decipher her sandwiches. One was stocked with peppery-tasting greens that probably had about as much nutritional value as grass. Mel devoured it and moved on. The next sandwich contained a sliver of smoked turkey, which vegetarian Mel would not eat. She longed to pluck the turkey out and eat the rest of the tomatoey, cheesy sandwich, but she had a feeling this would be considered very bad form.

And the final sandwich? Egg salad on pumpernickel.

Blech, Mel thought miserably. She moved on to her salad, dousing it with the inevitably fat-free dressing. Only when she was using the final radish slice to sop up the last drops of dressing did she remember—*whoops!* She should probably be listening to these introductions.

When Mel finally focused, one of the black-clad editors was talking. She pushed her bright green glasses farther up her nose and said, "I'm Lynn Stein, the photography editor. Which means, I'm currently juggling a feud between Carmelita and NaOmi, who—in case you've been living under a rock lately—are only the hottest, youngest, most petulent new supermodels on the scene. We want both of them to pose as sisters, the best of friends, on a June Cleaver-type set. Yeah, right. Models. Oy!"

A gorgeous woman with sky-high cheekbones and skin that glowed like polished mahogany cleared her throat and glared at the editor.

"Whoops," Stein said, though she looked thoroughly unperturbed. "I forgot our fashion editrix, the lovely Demetria Tish, used to be a model."

"A *super*model, if you must use the term," Demetria noted, looking like she enjoyed using the term very much, frankly. "The experience does come in handy."

Okay, drama queen much? Mel thought.

"Speaking of drama . . ."

Mel's eyes widened. A slender, blue-eyed man sitting opposite Lynn and Demetria had somehow managed to echo Mel's thoughts exactly.

". . . I'm Trey Narkisian, the entertainment editor," the man continued with a glint in his eye. "My department covers the stars of music, movies, and literature. Which, of course, includes the latest model-turned-whatever, because we all know how entertaining *they* are!"

Demetria's eyes narrowed to slits as Lynn barked out a distracted laugh. (She was making a note in her BlackBerry at the same time.)

Bishop gave Trey a long, cold stare that would have made Mel melt into her flip-flops. But Trey only coughed and huffed out, "Just a little joke, Demetria. You know I love you."

> **"And then she felt a buzzing in her brain. It wasn't at all a pleasant champagney buzz. It was more like the hum of a swarm of killer bees, aimed right for your head."**

Bishop released Trey from her icy blue eye-beams and glanced at the far end of the table.

"Last but not least," she announced, "is our managing editor, Quinn."

Quinn? Mel thought with a start. She followed Ms. Bishop's gaze down to the last chair on Mel's side of the table. Only when the chair's inhabitant stood up could Mel get a good look at him.

And then she felt a buzzing in her brain. It wasn't at all a pleasant champagney buzz. It was more like the hum of a swarm of killer bees, aimed right for your head. Mel felt a bright red flush travel from her hairline to somewhere around her knees.

"I'm Quinn Carson," said the man, running a hand over his perfect sweep of dark blond hair before resting it on his stubbled, chiseled chin. "Forgive my wrinkled suit. I just got off a plane from San Francisco."

Then Mel's hottie seatmate made eye contact with her, gave her a wink, and launched into his presentation.

Oh. My. God.

Mel felt a wave of nausea overtake her. Her skin prickled and her eyes went blurry. She couldn't blame the champagne (although its hazy aftereffects certainly didn't help). No, it was her shame spiral that was making her dizzy.

What have I done? she thought desperately.

ⓖ   ⓖ   ⓖ   ⓖ

The moment the luncheon ended, Mel whispered to Delia that she was desperate for a bathroom break. Scrutinizing Mel's face—which was no doubt pale and drawn after the whole humiliation-by-managing-editor—Delia nodded.

"Be back in five minutes. We're on a schedule," she said coolly.

Nodding vigorously, Mel rushed to the brushed-metal ladies' room door just outside the caf. Once she was safely locked in a stall, she unzipped her backpack and pulled out her journal. Flipping to a blank page, she scribbled:

First day performance evaluation . . .
 1) Got bubbly-drunk on plane
 2) Made ridiculous, possibly disparaging
  remarks about FLIRT to FLIRT's
  managing editor

3) Flirted with FLIRT's managing editor
4) Was late to my first-ever meeting at FLIRT
5) Showed up looking, let's just say, less than fresh
6) Emitted some sort of pheromone that caused FLIRT editor-in-chief to instantly hate me

Mel slapped her journal shut, took a deep breath, and left the stall. A Hudson-Bennetton was at the bathroom mirror, penciling a perfect, plum outline onto her lips. She glanced at Mel for less than a second before sniffing loudly and returning her attention to her impeccable face.

Flipping open her journal, Mel jotted down one more thing:

Yup, I've managed to make the worst impression I've ever made in my life—and I did it all before 2 p.m.

chapter two

After the meeting ended, Delia whisked the six interns out of the caf and gave the girls a whirlwind tour of the *Flirt* headquarters on the 22nd floor. As she walked down a long, somewhat drab hallway of offices with frosty-glassed doors, she ticked off the names of its inhabitants. Mel supposed she should recognize all the names—since they belonged to the editors who'd just introduced themselves at lunch. But beyond the department heads, the only name that was painfully familiar was Quinn Carson's.

One of the interns—the gorgeous, funky Asian girl—spoke up.

"Where is Ms. Bishop's office?" she asked.

"Unless you get the editorial internship, Kiyoko," Delia said, "you probably won't see much of Ms. Bishop's office. But FYI, it's at the other end of the hallway. In the corner."

"Duh," said the curly-haired girl who'd been whispering with her friend in the caf. Her brown eyes—heavily lined with liner and eye shadow—would have been pretty if they hadn't been half closed in disgust. "The editor-in-chief always has a corner office. Everybody knows that."

"Thanks, Genevieve," Delia said to the brown-eyed intern. "No one else here has the advantage of being Ms. Bishop's niece.

I'm sure the other girls will really appreciate it if you fill them in on all your *Flirt* trivia."

Mel squinted at Delia.

Do my ears deceive me, she wondered, *or was there a hint of snark in what Delia just said?*

Delia led the girls from the narrow hallway of offices into a sprawling network of cubicles, each stocked with a rolling chair and a flickering Mac. Genevieve's friend—a solidly built, sporty type—trotted along next to Genevieve, casting her a furtive smile at every opportunity.

Delia stalked to the far end of the cubicle farm and pointed at a cluster of six desks.

"Ladies," she said, "welcome to your home away from home. For now. Since you've already seen our famous caf, and now you know your way around the offices, let's get your paperwork filled out and your pictures taken for your ID badges. Then the driver will take you back to your loft. Or in the case of our latecomer . . ."

Delia shot Mel yet another judgmental look.

". . . to the loft for the first time."

Delia divided the group in half. She sent the first three off to a conference room to fill out temporary employee forms—Kiyoko, Genevieve, and Genevieve's friend, who was named Charlotte.

She gave Mel and the last two interns—Princess Di and the dark-haired überbabe—directions to the security office on the ground floor where they could get their ID badges made.

In the elevator, Mel finally had a chance to check out her last two roommates. They were both undisputedly gorgeous. The überbabe was about Mel's height, but twice as voluptuous.

"*Hola!*" the girl said, speaking up immediately. Her Latin accent was lilting and throaty all at once. "I'm Alexa. And this is Olivia."

"Hello," Olivia said with a little wave and a shy smile. *Her* accent was British. As much as Alexa was sexy and languid, Olivia was prim and proper. Her blond, chin-length hair was tucked neatly behind her ears. Mel couldn't help but notice that both girls had flawless manicures—Olivia's in pearly white and Alexa's in deep, dark red, with a slash of silver on each tip. Their makeup seemed pristine, too, right down to Alexa's berry lip gloss and Olivia's peachy pink cheeks.

"I'm Melanie," Mel said with a big smile. "But everybody calls me Mel."

"So sorry you had to rush from the airport," Olivia said sympathetically. The elevator landed in the lobby and the girls began to find their way to a hallway of offices. "I arrived from London yesterday. But luckily I was able to sleep off my jetlag before I even arrived. I just love the new seats on planes, don't you? The ones that convert into fully flat beds?"

"Um, actually, I've never experienced those," Mel said, her eyebrows raised.

"That's because you've probably never flown first-class across the ocean," Alexa whispered, with a wink. Then she turned to Olivia.

"*Cara,*" she said, "not all of us hail from Windsor Castle, you know. My parents are just humble college professors in Argentina."

"Hey!" Mel said. The girls had come upon a door with a plaque next to it that read Hudson-Bennett Security. "We're here."

The girls walked in and told the receptionist they needed their ID badges.

"Eh, the badge guy's on his break," the receptionist said, scratching her scalp with a pencil. "Have a seat. Be about fifteen minutes."

Shrugging, the girls plunked themselves into some vinyl chairs along the wall and kept on chatting.

"So, Mel?" Alexa said, giving her a plump-lipped smile. "What's your story?"

"Oh, I'm from Berkeley," Mel said, grinning back. "Um, that's in California. It's pretty much the crunch capital of the world."

"The what?" Olivia said with wide eyes. "Crunch?"

"You know," Mel said, giving Olivia's pale leg a nudge with her flip-flop. "Lots of patchouli, lots of granola . . ."

> "Lots of patchouli, lots of granola."

"The smell of hemp in the air . . ." Alexa said.

"You got it," Melanie confirmed with a laugh.

"As if," Alexa groaned. "Between my Catholic school and my completely intolerant parents, I'm lucky if I can get an hour a day to myself, much less the chance to do anything *bad*."

Mel could tell from the gleam in Alexa's eyes that *bad* was very good in her book.

"Unless," Alexa added, "you count taking your education into your own hands as something bad."

"Do tell," Mel said, slumping down in her seat. After the stressful morning, it felt good to relax.

"Let's just say," Alexa said, "that the 'family planning' video they show to absolutely every class, absolutely every year? It's a bit outdated. Hello, we're no longer interested in getting married at twenty-one and giving birth exactly nine months later, am I right? It's positively medieval. And I, for one, thought we should have a bit more realistic portrayal of the modern mating dance."

"Like?" Olivia said breathlessly.

"Like a Black Eyed Peas video," Alexa said, snorting with laughter. Mel joined in. Alexa was a scamp!

"Oh, you *are* bad," Olivia said to Alexa, giggling along with them. "What did your school do when you were caught?"

"They shipped me off to New York City," Alexa said with a shrug. "My principal thought this internship might teach me some responsibility. My *parents,* on the other hand, basically consider New York to be a gateway to cardinal sin."

"Not seriously?" Melanie laughed.

"Clearly, you don't have Argentine parents," Alexa said. "Back home, I don't have a curfew. Know why? Because I'm hardly ever allowed to go out unchaperoned! I go from home, to school, to the stables, and back home again. *Chiquitas*, it's like a prison."

"But now they've let you out!" Olivia announced.

"After *months* of begging," Alexa confirmed. "Plus two personal meetings with my school's principal and my art teacher, who told Mama and Papi that my photography talents should not be wasted. Finally, here I am. What do you Americans say? 'Free at last!'"

> **Finally, here I am. What do you Americans say? 'Free at last!'**

"I'm impressed," Mel said.

"I can't imagine what it's like to have parents like that," Olivia said. "I myself haven't seen either of my parents in over a month."

"What?" Alexa and Mel blurted together. They exchanged furtive glances.

"Well, I've been away at school," Olivia brushed off. "I'm from London, but my boarding school is in Wales. It's quite picturesque, actually. And during my break, my mum was in Italy, meeting with a new artist, and Daddy was . . . erm, actually, I don't remember where he was.

Isn't that funny?"

Mel thought it was kind of sad, actually. Even though her flight had left before dawn that morning, her entire family had gone with her to the airport—both her parents, her younger sister, and her two kid brothers. They'd buried her in so many hugs and good wishes that Mel had felt a little choked up as she'd headed to the security gate. As intent as she was to move onward and upward in life, a little part of her had wanted to take her chaotic family along with her.

"Doesn't that bother you? Not living with your family?" Mel asked Olivia, before it occurred to her that that wasn't the most sensitive question in the world.

"That's just the way my family operates," Olivia said. "My parents have an art gallery in Paris, which means they're constantly traveling about, wooing artists and such. Of course, we have a house in England, too. Well, my mum insists on calling it an estate, but I just think of it as home. It's in Hampstead Heath. My whole family loves it there, but sometimes it's difficult for us all to land there at the same time. I guess that must seem mad to you?"

Mel was about to dispute that fact when a round-bellied man in a khaki security uniform sauntered into the office.

"Hey, Artie," the receptionist said to him. "We got a few girls here who need their ID badges."

Artie sized the three interns up.

"Okay," he said, "I guess none of you's will break the camera lens. Who's up first?"

⟲   ⟲   ⟲   ⟲

It was four o'clock before all the interns' business was squared away. By then, Mel was limp with exhaustion and grateful when Delia told their sextet to head home.

"Come on," Genevieve declared, leading the girls down a narrow hallway, away from the elevators clustered near the receptionist. "I can take us to the express elevator."

The elevator was tucked close to Bishop's office and Genevieve seemed inordinately proud to know about its existence. Once it had whizzed the girls down to the lobby, Genevieve led their troupe out to the street.

The Hudson-Bennett building was in Midtown. And Midtown was all about stony buildings whose peaked caps hid in the clouds. Its wide sidewalks were crammed with people in suits, ladies walking tiny dogs on glittery leashes, and wide-eyed tourists wondering aloud how to find the Empire State Building.

The loft where the six girls would be living for the summer was downtown, in SoHo. Jared was waiting by the curb to take them there.

As he drove the limo south, Mel opened the backseat window to peer outside. With each passing block, she became more certain that downtown was *her* kind of town. The streets grew more narrow, and Mel began to see more leafy trees. The buildings here were shorter, and many were adorned with lacy balconies, stony gargoyles, or scrolly ramparts. The people strolling the streets seemed to be funkier and hipper with each passing block.

"I love how *alive* everything is in New York," Olivia burbled, peeking out the window with Mel. "It makes England seem so fusty. My family's country home is older than this entire country, would you believe? Castles that go back six hundred years are quite common over there."

> **"I love how alive everything is in New York."**

"Cali's just a baby compared to your hometown," Mel laughed. She turned to Genevieve, Kiyoko, and Charlotte. "By the way, where are you guys from?"

For the rest of the car ride, the girls went through their histories. Genevieve and Charlotte both lived in Connecticut and went to the same hoity private school.

"Of course," Genevieve said with a sniff, "I've lived in New York before. I was an intern last summer! Aunt Josephine made it clear that I just *had* to come back for a second run."

"Really?" Charlotte said. Her voice was high and squeaky. "I thought you had to *beg* your aunt for this internsh—"

"Oh my God," Genevieve interrupted her neatly.

She pointed out the window. "Check it out! It's Jake Gyllenhaal!"

"What? Lemme see!" the other girls squealed, scrambling to get a good view out the window.

All except Kiyoko.

"Not even, lads," she scoffed. "He's filming a movie in Berlin. I read about it in a gossip mag on the plane. I mean, we *will* see some celebs this summer," Kiyoko went on knowingly. "New York is crawling with 'em. Man, it's good to finally be here. I've lived seriously *everywhere*. But New York I've yet to conquer."

"Everywhere. Really?" Olivia said, with a polite smile. "Where else have you lived?"

"Oh, you name it," Kiyoko began.

"All right," Olivia said. "Paris, Gstaad, Monaco, Johannesburg?"

"Try Dublin, Rio, London, Paris, Rome, Lisbon, Vienna, and Zurich," Kiyoko breezed back. "And of course, Tokyo, where I was born. I guess being a diplomat's daughter even trumps being one of the famous Bourne-Cecils, huh?"

"What does that mean?" Olivia said. She seemed taken aback.

"Nothing," Kiyoko said, sounding bored with the conversation. "It's just that—like anybody who's read *Tatler*—I've heard of the insanely rich, highborn Bourne-Cecils. I guess it was the fact that Bishop and your mother were boarding-school mates that got you this gig?"

"Well," Olivia breathed, going pale, "it is true that Mum and Ms. Bishop are old friends, but I hardly think that means . . ."

"Sure it doesn't," Kiyoko said. Then she smiled. "Don't mind me, Liv. I'm just playing."

But Olivia looked anything but playful. She chewed on her lip some more and hung her head, staring for a moment at her own demurely crossed ankles.

"Hey, guys," Mel laughed. "Save the competition for *Flirt*, huh?"

Olivia and Kiyoko barely acknowledged her, but Genevieve pounced on Mel's subject change.

"The competition starts tomorrow," she pointed out. "We get our internship assignments then. Each of us will go to one department. *I* fully intend to be in the editorial department. I've been writing pieces for my school paper since I was a freshman."

Mel bit her lip. She was dying for the editorial assignment, too. In fact, she'd just assumed it was already hers, since she'd emphasized her writing talent in her *Flirt* application. She couldn't believe it hadn't occurred to her that she'd still be jockeying for position even after being awarded the internship.

If Mel had been a broody type, she'd be getting ready for some serious hand-wringing right now.

But a) she wasn't, and b) Jared had just pulled the limo up to a curb on a narrow, cobblestone street in SoHo. Intent on beating the driver to the royal treatment,

Mel grabbed her door handle and jumped out onto the street. Before she could orient herself, a pizza delivery guy on a Vespa zipped by, coming dangerously close to mowing Mel down.

"Hey, watch it!" the scooter boy screamed at her as he screeched to a halt and glared over his shoulder at her.

"Ooh, sorry!" Mel said.

The guy's scowl slowly turned into a smile.

"Eh, don't sweat it, beautiful," he called back. Then he kick-started his scooter again and zipped away.

Alexa climbed out of the limo after Mel.

"I think somebody likes you," she teased.

"Well, at least *somebody* does," Mel shrugged. "Since Ms. Bishop clearly thinks I'm a reject."

"Don't let Genevieve hear you say that," Kiyoko whispered as she clambered out of the limo after them.

"Why?" Mel queried.

"Hello?" Kiyoko said. "You don't think she has it out for the rest of us?"

"Really?" Mel said. "But Genevieve just met me! And she's only known you guys for twenty-four hours. Why would she have it out for us? I bet she's just a little tense, that's all. You know—nervous about pleasing her aunt this summer."

"You're more trusting than I," Kiyoko muttered.

"I guess I'm of the trustworthy-until-proven-untrustworthy school." Mel smiled.

Then she spun around, joyfully taking in the beauty that was SoHo. She gazed up at the building before them. Each of its windows looked at least eight feet tall. "Which one is ours?"

"The top one," Alexa said as Jared hauled Mel's duffel out of the trunk. "Wait'll you see it!"

"The whole top floor, of course," Genevieve sniffed, having just climbed out of the limo to join the crew.

"Yup," Jared said with a grin. "Everybody else in New York lives in a shoe box, but for the Hudson-Bennett interns? A loft the size of a football field. During the winter months, the mag rents it out to their favorite fashion models."

"It's totally gonna be like *The Real World*," Kiyoko said, happily fishing Mel's backpack out of the trunk. "You know, that ancient season from New York? We're gonna party all the time, lads!"

"Oh, please," Olivia dismissed. "We'll be working too hard for all that."

"What-*ever*," Kiyoko huffed. "Can't a girl dream?"

Mel grabbed her duffel from Jared with a grateful smile, then barreled between her sparring roomies.

"Coming through!" she called cheerfully. "You've all spent a night in this famous loft already, but *I'm* dying to see it!"

Mel plunged through the front door and skidded to a halt in front of yet another reception desk. Behind it was a wiry young guy whose eyes were glued to a tiny TV.

He carefully hit pause on the tube's built-in VCR, then turned a sunny smile on Mel.

"You must be the last intern," he exclaimed. "We've been waiting!"

He pushed an intercom button on his desk.

"Emma?" he said. "It's Sammy. The interns are here! All six of 'em."

"That's our house mother, right?" Mel said to Alexa.

"Yeah," Alexa said. "She's nice. I mean, for an authority figure."

The girls led Mel to a craggy, industrial elevator, which ferried them directly into their top-floor loft.

As soon as the elevator door opened, Mel gasped.

She'd seen museum galleries that weren't half the size of the loft's main room. The space felt like an endless swath of exposed brick, interrupted here and there by distressed concrete pillars.

One wall consisted of nothing but arched, multipaned windows. On the far left side of the loft was a sunken living room area containing a cozy assemblage of couches, chairs, shaggy rugs, and bookshelves. To the right of the elevator, an open kitchen featured a funky

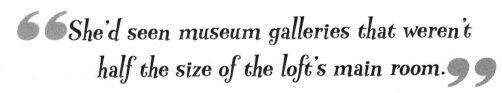

She'd seen museum galleries that weren't half the size of the loft's main room.

'50s-era fridge and an equally retro stove. A long, rustic dining table floated outside the kitchen. Its colorful mismatched chairs somehow went perfectly with the rest of the loft's urban starkness.

Finally, on the far right side of the space, a twisty wrought-iron staircase led up to several doorways, which Mel assumed were bedrooms. The hallway next to these rooms, Mel supposed, led to yet more magic.

From that hallway, a slim, graceful woman emerged. She wore Birkenstocks, flappy linen pants, and a spaghetti strap tank that showed off her slender, freckled arms. Her long, amber-colored hair was gathered into an artfully sloppy ponytail and her sun-kissed face was makeup free.

"Hey, guys," she said. Her wide smile revealed a cute gap between her front teeth. Mel liked her immediately, and the feeling seemed to be mutual when she took Mel's hand.

"I'm Emma Lyric," she said. "Ms. Bishop calls me your housemother, but I prefer resident advisor. Y'know, like they have in college dorms? It's a little more grown-up, eh?"

As she spoke, she headed to the kitchen and grabbed a white cardboard box tied with red-and-white string.

"I picked up some cream puffs from this little place down the street," she said, plunking the box on the table with a stack of chipped, mismatched dessert plates.

Then she went to the fridge and pulled out a pitcher of lemonade. "I know there's no such thing as dessert in the oh-so-austere Hudson-Bennett cafeteria, so I thought you all might have a taste for something sweet after your first day."

Genevieve sniffed at the treats.

"No thanks," she said, skimming a hand over her slender hips. "I'm on the Zone. It's a modeling thing."

"Uh, Gen?" Kiyoko noted, sizing Genevieve up with a quick glance. "Isn't height a modeling thing, too? You look to be about five feet six inches or so. My sister Miko's doing the mannequin thing in London this summer, and she says the agencies won't even look at you if you're under five foot ten. She's almost six feet, herself."

Genevieve gave Kiyoko a fiery look, then turned on her heel and stomped toward the bedroom on the far side of the loft's balcony—the only one with windows.

> **I'd be crabby, too, if I skipped dessert.**

"I'd be crabby, too," Mel said, licking the last of her cream puff off her fingers, "if I skipped dessert. Hey, those are the bedrooms up there, right? Which one's mine?"

Kiyoko had been glaring at Genevieve's retreating back, but now she turned to Mel, an uncomfortable grimace on her face.

"Well, you see . . ." she began.

"We're sharing rooms," Olivia cut in. She looped her arm through Mel's, leading her to one of the couches on the other side of the loft. Alexa and Kiyoko followed while Emma lagged behind in the dining room. "Emma had already made our roommate assignments when we arrived and . . ."

Olivia cast a careful glance at Kiyoko and Alexa.

"I'm sharing with Kiyoko," Alexa announced bluntly. "And Olivia's with Charlotte. Which leaves you to room with—"

"Genevieve," Mel said. She looked at her new friends' long, sympathetic faces. "You guys, that's fine! I swear, I don't think Genevieve's that bad. She's just a little type A, that's all. Maybe rooming with a type B like myself all summer will loosen her up."

"Ladies," Kiyoko said drily. "I think we've found the Flirt-cave's ray of sunshine."

Emma appeared behind the girls and grinned.

"Then I guess Mel won't have a problem with some of our other house rules," she said. "The main one is curfew. Eleven o'clock on weeknights and midnight on weekends." She pointed at a bookshelf next to the elevator. "Over there you'll find a subway map you should stash in your bag, along with one of the cards I've printed up with all our emergency phone numbers. There are also travel guides to New York, takeout menus, and whatever else you might need to navigate your way around our big burg for eight weeks."

" This is definitely the best place I've ever lived! "

"For now," Mel sighed happily, "I just want to navigate this mega loft!"

She stretched out across the couch and gazed across the expansive loft. It was so vast that she had a sudden urge to run a lap around it.

Feeling a devilish grin erupt on her face, Mel sprang out of her seat and hurried over to her duffel, which she'd tossed to the floor just inside the elevator door. Unzipping the bag, she plopped onto the floor and began to rifle through her clothes, paperback books, loose toiletries, and the other ephemera she'd tossed into her bag the previous night. Finally, she found what she was looking for.

Two minutes later, Mel hauled herself to her feet. Or, to be more precise, to the wheels of the Rollerblades she'd just strapped on. With a little whoop, she set off, gliding across the endless hardwood floor. She did a few neat crossovers to skate around the collection of couches, then headed back toward the girls. Lifting one leg behind her, Mel dipped into a graceful spiral and declared, "This is definitely the best place I've ever lived!"

"Which means maybe you'd prefer *not* to turn it into a skating rink?" Emma called after her.

Mel winked at the girls' "resident advisor" as she did a tight loop around the dining table, then picked up some speed to do one more glide around the room. Somehow the airiness of the giant windows, the high ceilings with their exposed wooden beams, and the glossy floor was even prettier when seen from skates. After all the snafus of the day, finally Mel felt free—speedy, graceful, and ready to take on New Yo—

Crash!

"Aigh!" Mel screamed. She'd hit something! And she'd hit it so hard that she went careening to the floor. She lay on the floor for a moment, her eyes closed, listening to her skate wheels *zzzzz* to a halt. Then she heard something else.

Something that made her heart stop.

"Owwwwww," a voice groaned.

Mel's eyes snapped open. She hadn't hit *something*. She'd hit *someone*. She struggled to a sitting position—wincing at some brand-new bruises—and gaped at the someone.

He was sitting on the floor just outside the elevator door. Clearly, he'd arrived in the loft about half a second before Mel made impact with him. He was rubbing his ribs, his face contorted with surprise and pain.

As the interns and Emma ran over, Mel dazedly registered a few things about the person she'd just greeted so rudely.

1) He was a *he*.
2) He was young. Mel didn't know how young, but she was willing to bet he was *just* old enough

to vote.

3) He was gorgeous. As the guy rubbed his ribs, Mel could clearly see some very nice muscles beneath his slouchy/cool T-shirt. His legs, clad in nicely dirtied-up jeans, were superlong, meaning he was probably taller than Mel by at least a few inches. He had a nice square chin, a small nose with the cutest of bumps on the bridge, and long-lashed, chocolate brown eyes. In fact, his eyes were the same shade as Emma's.

Which must mean—Mel realized in horror.

"Uh, Mel?" Emma said as she knelt down next to them. "Meet my son, Nicholas."

"Oh my God," Mel groaned. "I'm so sorry, Nicholas! Are you okay?"

"It's Nick, usually," the guy said, looking up to meet Mel's eyes for the first time. He gave her a good-natured grin. "And yeah, I think I'm fine. But next time I come home you could just say, 'Hi, honey, how was your day?' "

Nick pulled himself to his feet and extended a hand to help Mel up—which gave her the opportunity to note how nice and big and strong his hands were.

Suddenly Mel felt herself going bubbly inside. But this time, champagne had nothing to do with it.

"Hi, honey, how was your day?" she asked, smiling.

Nick grinned and quipped back, "Oh, you know,

the usual. Got mowed down by a cab or two. Collided with a bicycle messenger. Then came home just in time to catch the Roller Derby."

Mel giggled helplessly. "You *live* here?" she said.

While Nick nodded, Emma explained. "Nick and I have a suite at the end of that long hallway. We live there and both have art studios there."

"So you're an artist?" Mel breathed to Nick.

"Well," Nick shrugged, "student artist, anyway. I just finished my freshman year at NYU. So I'm home for the summer, y'know, waiting tables by day, playing with my paints at night."

"Cool," Mel said.

"Do you paint, too, Emma?" Olivia asked.

"Me?" Emma said. "Nah. I'm a photographer. I was a *Flirt* fashion photographer, once upon a time. Now I'm onto artier stuff, but *Flirt* kept me on as, you know . . ."

"Housemother," all the interns singsonged with a laugh.

"Wait a minute," Nick said as he ambled over to the dining table and grabbed himself a cream puff. "If she's a housemother, what does that make me? House brother?"

Oh, I hope not, Mel thought with a sly grin.

⊙　　⊙　　⊙　　⊙

Mel didn't come back to earth until she'd unpacked

all her things in her room. Genevieve had already taken the bed farthest from the window, so Mel got the mattress with a view.

She shoved her clothes into her small closet, propped pictures of her family on her dresser, and added a little atmosphere by draping a tie-dyed scarf over her bedside lamp. Then she made her bed with a quilt her grandmother had stitched up for her when Mel was a little girl.

Genevieve's side of the room, in addition to being shaded from the morning sun, was organized to a T. She'd arranged pillow shams on the bed that exactly matched her ice blue duvet, and color coded all the outfits in her closet.

"Wow," Mel said, eyeing Genevieve's impeccable stuff. "You really *are* Josephine Bishop's niece, aren't you?"

"Well," Genevieve said lightly, "I've learned that success is all about presentation. If you *look* together, you probably *are* together."

She gave Mel's still-frowsy hair and rumpled clothes a pointed once-over.

Mel shrugged.

I'm sure, Mel assured herself, *when I get to know Gen better, I'll get her sense of humor.*

Before she could give it any more thought, Kiyoko poked her head into the bedroom. She'd changed into skintight, whiskery jeans and a tank top emblazoned with some goofy cartoon characters. Her hot pink mascara matched her bubble-gum-colored wristbands.

"Hey, girlfriends," she said, though she was only looking at Mel. "Ready for our first night on the town?"

She held up a dog-eared copy of *Time Out New York*.

"I know just where to go!" she said. By now, Olivia, Charlotte, and Alexa had crowded into the doorway behind her. "Bowlmor Lanes! It's this rad bowling alley near Union Square."

Mel glanced at the thick orientation folder on her nightstand. It lay on top of a tall stack of *Flirt*s, which Mel had brought from home to study.

Maybe, she realized, *I should start my self-improvement plan tonight.*

> **Mel, work can wait! It's our first night all together in the big city!**

"Bowlmor sounds fab," Mel said regretfully. "But I'm wiped, you guys. I think I'm gonna stay here and do a little reading. I totally zoned during that orientation meeting so I've got to catch up."

"Aw, are you sure?" Alexa said. She, too, had changed out of her work clothes. She was wearing a halter-topped dress with a sweeping skirt that made the most of her curvy hips. "Mel, work can wait! It's our first night all together in the big city!"

Alexa spun around and did a few swivelly dance moves to emphasize her point.

Mel laughed. Alexa and Kiyoko were so fun. And Olivia and Charlotte seemed so sweet. Mel was sorely tempted to join them for their night out.

But an instant later, she shook her head.

For once, she decided, *I can't flake. This internship is too important to blow on day one.*

"Yeah, I'm sure," Mel told Alexa, settling back on her bed and picking up her folder. "You guys have fun."

Mel was just flipping the folder open and waving good-bye to her roomies as they shuffled their way out when a new voice piped up just outside the door.

It was a male voice—one she already recognized.

"You're going to Bowlmor?" Nick said to the girls from just outside Mel's room. "That place is sweet! Mind if I tag along?"

Mel froze. Almost against her will, she felt herself slap the folder closed. Then she bounced off the bed and announced, "You know what? I think you're right. Our first night all together in the city deserves to be celebrated. I think I'll go with you after all!"

chapter three

Within fifteen minutes, Mel found herself squeezed into the *Flirt* limo with her five roommates—and Nick.

In the five minutes she'd had to totally change her mind and get ready before they'd left for Bowlmor, Mel had pulled her hair out of its elastic and run her fingers through the long, blond waves. Then she'd shimmied out of her wrinkled skirt and tank and hopped into a slightly less wrinkled pair of skintight denims, along with a shimmery halter top and some strappy, kitten-heeled mules.

She'd wished she could slap some blue polish onto her toenails or comb some mascara onto her long, gold lashes. But with no time for that, she'd merely splashed the day's grime off her face, swiped some peach gloss onto her lips, and shrugged at herself in the bathroom mirror before walking out to join her friends.

"Oh la la!" Kiyoko had cried. *"Très magnifique!"*

"Yeah," Genevieve admitted, skimming a finger over her own perfectly lined lips. "You clean up okay, Mel. Now, if you only knew anything about makeup, maybe you could get the Beauty internship at *Flirt*."

"A of all," Kiyoko had retorted, *"some* people don't need

makeup. And B, I don't think the beauty gig is Mel's bag."

She was eyeing Mel's journal, which Mel had stuffed into the back pocket of her jeans, along with her purple pen. Mel could bet that Kiyoko had already pegged her as a writer.

"Hey," Mel had said, eager to change the subject. "Are we gonna head out, or what?"

So now they were in the limo. Mel felt a twinge of regret that she hadn't landed in the backseat next to Nick. Instead, he was sandwiched between Alexa and Genevieve. Genevieve was smiling sweetly at him.

Oh well, Mel consoled herself from her seat across from Nick. *At least from here I have a direct view of his beautiful face.*

"It was so nice of *Flirt*," Olivia said, "to provide us with car service, wasn't it? I don't know *what* I'd do if I had to navigate my own way around New York all summer. I'm hopeless with directions."

Nick and Jared, the driver, both laughed.

"Um, Olivia?" Nick said gently. "You know when my mom gave you a subway map earlier?"

"Yes," Olivia squeaked. "What of it?"

"You might want to study up on that," Nick said. "This limo thing? It's just a welcome-to-*Flirt* present."

"Expiration date," Jared called over his shoulder, "the minute I drop you guys off at that crazy bowling alley. It's been fun, kiddies, but after this, I go back to shuttling Hudson-Bennett executives and petulant fashion models."

"Oh, but you *know* we're more fun," Kiyoko teased.

"Them's the rules, little girl," Jared laughed.

"Little girl!" Kiyoko squeaked. She began bobbling one of her high-heeled feet indignantly. "Even my *parents* don't think of me as a little girl."

But before Kiyoko could work herself into a mood, the limo pulled up to the curb.

Mel was the last of the crew to climb out of the car.

"Good luck with your summer, kid," Jared said as he held the door for her. "Or should I say *lady*? I think I made Kiyoko mad!"

"Call me kid anytime," Mel said, giving Jared a hug. "And thanks for the luck. I need it!"

☺   ☺   ☺   ☺

Like the loft, Bowlmor was a kooky combo of retro and mod. The entry was lit by funky pink neon, but the image that greeted guests was a demure woman in a '50s bouffant wielding a lavender bowling ball.

Inside, the place was huge—an ocean of alleys fronted by cozy, bright blue booths. Behind it all was a Jetsons-style bar—a glossy boomerang of blond wood, blue vinyl stools, and an industrial mesh ceiling. The music vacillated between metallic techno and goofy disco songs by ABBA.

After her plane trip, the biggest kick Mel wanted from the bar was some caffeine. But Kiyoko had other ideas. From the moment she stepped foot in Bowlmor, she looked ready to conquer it. She stood at the edge of the bar area, her hands on her sharp hip bones, her chin angled with attitude. She waited for the inevitable head swivels.

And what do you know—a couple of guys sitting at the bar obliged her. They raised their foamy glasses of beer at Kiyoko in a salute before returning to their conversation.

"Bingo," Kiyoko whispered while Olivia covered her mouth with her hand to laugh shyly. "Those guys so want me."

She, of course, couldn't have cared less about them. She had her eye on a different man.

The bartender.

She flung a hank of impossibly shiny black hair over her skinny shoulder and batted her pink eyelashes at her buds.

> *After her plane trip, the biggest kick Mel wanted from the bar was some caffeine. But Kiyoko had other ideas.*

"I'm going to go show these guys who's a 'little girl,' " she declared. "I'll meet you at our lane?"

Now it was Charlotte who was giggling.

"Hey," she whispered to Kiyoko. "While you're over there, could you get me a rum and Coke?"

"Not a chance, lad," Kiyoko breezed. "Rum and Coke is *so* bridge and tunnel. Now, if you want a pomegranate sojutini . . ."

"You just go work it, girlfriend," Mel laughed. "We'll get set up. What's your shoe size?"

"Eight and a half," Kiyoko said. In a seamless motion, she kicked up one heel, sending her high-heeled mule floating into the air. She caught it neatly, flipped off her other shoe, then handed both of them to Mel. "You can trade these in for my bowling shoes. Meanwhile, I've got a bartender to tease mercilessly."

She winked at her friends, spun around, and slunk over to the bar, her flirty purpose diminished not at all by the fact that she was strutting in bare feet.

"We know Kiyoko's ready for New York," Mel laughed to the rest of the group as they headed for the shoe-rental counter. "But is New York ready for her?!"

◎   ◎   ◎   ◎

When their crew was set up at a bowling lane, Alexa pointed out, "With a group this big, we better split into teams. Olivia? Want to be my partner?"

"Oh, I'll make you lose," Olivia said. "I'm sure I'm rubbish."

"I'm sure I am, too!" Alexa laughed. "We don't even have bowling in Argentina. But I love to try new things. Like the time back home that I snuck out of the house and hitchhiked with some girlfriends to an all-night rave. *That* was a fun first time, too!"

"*You,*" Mel said, pointing at Alexa with a grin, "are so going to get us into trouble this summer."

"Let us hope, *chica,*" Alexa cackled. "Let us hope."

Genevieve wasn't laughing. She was giving Nick a sidelong glance.

"I'll team up," she began, "with Ni—"

"Me!" Charlotte blurted, planting herself at Genevieve's side. She smiled widely at Genevieve.

Genevieve gritted her teeth but nodded stiffly at Charlotte. Then she busied herself with typing their names into the computer scorekeeper in the middle of their booth.

Nick turned to Mel.

"I guess that leaves you and me," he said—with a sweet smile.

"I guess so," Mel said warmly. *Oh, well.*

"And Kiyoko!" Genevieve provided with a simpering smile. She glanced beyond Mel. Kiyoko was stalking toward them, a glass of something clear and fizzy in her hand and a scowl on her face.

"Kiyoko," Nick said. "Want to be on me and Mel's team?"

"Sure, whatever," Kiyoko muttered.

"No pomegranate sojutinis?" Mel said sympathetically. "What's that? A vodka tonic?"

> **I mean, hello? Check out the merch!**

"Try *just* tonic," Kiyoko grumbled with a curled lip. "The dude wouldn't serve me. He must be blind. I mean, hello? Check out the merch!"

Kiyoko gave her black hair an emphatic flip.

"Let's bowl," Nick said with a wry smile. He passed Kiyoko her shoes. "And by the way, I think those guys two lanes over are drooling in your direction."

"Really?" Kiyoko said slyly. She peeked over at the guys, who were indeed smiling at their lane. Mel couldn't tell whether they were making eyes at Kiyoko specifically, or at the interns in general. But Kiyoko clearly thought the gazes were all for her.

"Back in the game," she whispered. "Now let's get bowling already."

"Right, well, I'm not so sure about that part," Olivia said, looking a little pale. She was holding up one of her red, white, and blue bowling shoes with her thumb and forefinger. "You guys? I think my shoes are *used.*"

"Kinda comes with the territory," Charlotte said as she laced on her shoes.

"Oh?" Olivia said. "So, that's how bowling works?"

"Yup," Mel said, tying on her own shoes. "They're rental shoes. Which is a blessing, when you think about it. I mean, you wouldn't want to have to *keep* 'em!"

"Heh, heh," Olivia laughed nervously. "All right then . . ."

She kicked off one of her black-and-white spectator pumps and got ready to slip on one of the bowling shoes. But just before her bare toes hit the saggy, somewhat fragrant leather, she hesitated.

"You know," she quavered, "*my* shoes are so comfortable, do you think it would be all right if I wore my own?"

"Hey, whatever floats your boat," Kiyoko said. She strode up to the carousel in front of their lane and hoisted up a hot pink bowling ball that matched her accessories. "As long as you don't get busted. But while you're going on about footwear, *I'm* going to get this game started."

She held the ball up in front of her face, glanced at the boys two lanes over, who were still ogling her, and executed the most sinuous, sexy bowl Mel had ever seen.

"Strike!" Nick yelled.

Olivia put a finger to her chin.

"So you just trot up to the line and toss it?" she asked her friends.

"Well, there are nuances to it," Nick added. "You know, angle and spin and follow-through and stuff like that. But tell you what, Olivia. We'll get to that some other bowling night. For now, just trot and toss."

In three-inch spectator pumps, that was clearly easier said

> ❝ **For now, just trot and toss.** ❞

than done. Olivia selected a smallish purple ball but still grunted as she picked it up. Weighed down by the heavy bowling ball, Olivia's trot was more of a clomp. And the toss? Well, somehow Olivia's fingers got stuck in the holes, and when she threw her ball, she went down with it.

"Oh my God!" Mel and Alexa cried, running to Olivia's aid.

"Are you okay?" Alexa said.

"Just embarrassed is all," Olivia said, glancing around. When she tried to walk back to their booth, she almost fell again. Gasping, she looked down at her right foot.

Her black-and-white heel was dangling off the end of her shoe.

"Oh, crikey!" Olivia said. "Now how am I going to walk around the rest of the night?"

"And look what's happened to your pretty, pretty shoe," Alexa lamented. "Maybe Emma can tell us about a shoe repair shop."

"Oh, I suppose," Olivia said as she limped back to her seat. "I'm not sure I should bother, though. These shoes were only about two hundred pounds."

Mel skidded to a halt.

"Olivia!" she squawked. "That's like three hundred and fifty American dollars!"

"Is . . . is that a lot?" Olivia asked.

"For some of us!" Alexa exclaimed.

"Dudes," Genevieve yelled. "Olivia hasn't taken her second shot!"

Alexa pointed at Olivia's ailing shoe and volunteered. "I'll take it for her."

"I don't know if that's allowed." Genevieve frowned. "Teammates should take turns, not—"

"Do any of you object?" Alexa asked, glancing at the others.

"Go for it," Mel said.

"If you say so," Alexa said with a mischievous grin. She selected a cherry red ball, then skimmed up to the bowling alley's line. But she didn't stop there. Shimmying her hips to the disco music pumping through the joint, she danced right up the lane. When she was only about ten feet away from the pyramid of pins, she bent over at the waist, plunked her ball on the floor, and pushed it into the pins, knocking down every one.

"Alexa!" Olivia cried, slapping her hands to her cheeks. "I don't think you're supposed to do that!"

But the rest of their group was laughing so hard, they couldn't say anything. Bowlers in nearby lanes, particularly male ones, clapped and cheered for Alexa's little performance.

The only people who were *not* amused were a couple of guys in vintage-style Bowlmor logo shirts. They stalked up to the interns, their arms crossed angrily over their chests.

"Oh, Alexa?" Genevieve called out as Alexa bowed to her fans. "I think someone wants to have a little talk with you."

Instead of freaking, Alexa immediately plastered a wide-eyed, innocent smile on her face.

"*Oh, lo siento. ¿Tenemos un problema?*" she cooed.

"Um . . . what?" one of the burly guys grunted.

"*En mi país, así es cómo jugamos a los bolos,*" Alexa went on, batting her long eyelashes.

"Pardon me, boys," Kiyoko said, fluttering her own pink lashes as she stepped between the security thugs and Alexa. "But I'm fluent in Spanish. And what this girl is saying is that this is how they bowl in her country. She had no idea she wasn't supposed to. She's dreadfully sorry."

Alexa clasped her hands and put on a penitent expression.

Mel, meanwhile, was biting the insides of both her cheeks to keep from guffawing out loud. She could feel her face turning red, too.

Suddenly, she felt something else—Nick's breath on her ear.

"I think Alexa just may squeak out of this situation,"

he whispered. "That is, *if* we keep it together."

"I know!" Mel squeaked under her breath. "But it's just. So. Funny!"

"C'mon," Nick said, getting to his feet. "Let's go somewhere else. We can get a drink at the bar."

Covering her mouth to hold in her laughter, Mel lurched to her feet and followed Nick.

"Be back in a minute, guys," Nick said to the others.

The moment Mel and Nick bellied up to the bar, Mel lost it. She grabbed her middle and guffawed for a full minute.

While she hiccuped out the last of her giggles, Nick waved at the bartender.

"Coke, please," Mel gasped, wiping tears from her eyes as her laughs finally died down.

"Diet Coke," the bartender said briskly, turning to Nick. "And for you?"

"No, actually, I want regular Coke," Mel requested. "And if you can throw a couple maraschino cherries in there, that would be cool."

Nick raised his eyebrows at her.

"What?" Mel shrugged. "I like my sugar."

Nick grinned.

"Sorry," he said. "It's just, New York girls only drink diet."

"I'm not from New York," Mel teased.

Nick ordered a Coke for himself and said to Mel,

"You're from Berkeley, right?"

"Yes. I hail from the land of wheatgrass and Birkenstocks," Mel said. She glanced at Kiyoko, Olivia, and Alexa over at the bowling alley. "I'm not nearly as exotic as our international buds over there."

"Oh, I don't know about that," Nick said.

Nick's comment gave Mel a jolt that a Coke could never match, but she tried not to let it show.

"What about you?" she said. "Have you always lived in New York?"

"Born and raised," Nick said. "My parents got married here really young. Split up really young, too."

"Oh, I'm sorry," Mel said.

"Nah, it's okay," Nick said. "I mean, the folks did a good job of it. They got divorced when I was a baby and I didn't know the difference, and they still get along really well. Basically, my mom is much happier being on her own. She's not your average, chicken-roasting, settled-down mom type."

"So I noticed," Mel said, taking a slurp of her soda. "I have to say, I think she's beyond cool."

"Yeah, I lucked out," Nick admitted. "We have a good time, kicking around the loft and talking art and stuff. I guess we're a lot alike, my mom and me. I'm pretty independent."

"Oh, me too," Mel nodded. "I mean, why else would I ditch my family—not to mention Berkeley—for the whole summer? I gotta be me."

Could this day be any crazier? she asked herself. *I went from being on top of the world—literally—to feeling like gum on Josephine Bishop's shoe, to lounging in a New York bar/bowling alley with the cutest boy I've ever seen in real life. I can't wrap my brain around all this!*

Mel's long, slender fingers crept to her back pocket. The top of her journal was just peeking out of it. She knew if anything would help her process all the stuff that happened that day, it was a quick scribble in her diary.

"Hey, guys," said a voice behind them. Mel spun around on her bar stool. Charlotte smiled at them shyly.

"Genevieve asked me to grab some drinks," she explained. "Alexa and Kiyoko not only talked those guys into letting us stay, they finagled some free soda coupons out of them, too."

Charlotte giggled as she showed Mel and Nick a sheaf of Bowlmor drink coupons.

Now it was Nick who laughed and laughed.

"That's a lot of free drinks," he exclaimed. "I'll help you carry them."

"Cool," Mel said. She grinned and slid off her seat. Charlotte had given her the perfect opening to take a journal break. "I'll leave that to you guys while I hit the restroom."

In the ladies room, she hoisted herself onto the counter, whipped out her journal, and started writing . . .

Nick + Mel scenarios—Options:

1) We could tap-dance around each other for the entire summer, because it's probably not kosher to date your "housemother's" son. Only on my last night in New York City would our passion overtake us. We'd finally exchange a legendary kiss and promise that next summer, we'd be together.
Pro: Completely romantic
Con: Deferred gratification.
Grade: C

2) We could declare our like-like for each other THIS VERY NIGHT. But then, after a couple of weeks of dating AND cohabitation, we would start grating on each other. I'd see him flossing in the kitchen, for instance. Or he'd run into me in the morning en route to the bathroom and realize what I look like with bedhead. The fizz would fizzle and the rest of the summer would be Majorly. Awkward. For everyone!
Pro: Well, at least I would get to kiss Nick tonight!
Con: Things could get Majorly. Awkward.
Grade: D

3) We could be friends—hang-out buddies who do cool stuff together like scrounging antique stores and sampling every single gelato flavor at Ciao Bella, that cute ice-cream shop I spotted just down the street from the loft. As we pal around, we'll realize that deep down, we're in love. Our friendship will stay fabulous, but we'll ALSO be boyfriend-girlfriend!
Pro: I could write a screenplay based on our relationship and sell it to Hollywood.
Con: I already know I have a crush on Nick! So this scenario can't really work. Unless I . . . sort of . . . forgot? It could happen.
Grade: B+

4) We find ourselves locked in a walk-in freezer together. Where this will occur, I have no idea. The point is—

"Mel!"

Mel's purple pen skittered off the edge of her page. She glanced up to see Olivia poking her head through the bathroom door, looking bewildered.

"Have you been in here all this time?" Olivia sputtered.

"Um," Mel said. She glanced at the two pages of

her journal she'd just filled. "I guess I lost track of time."

"Good thing I had to go to the loo, then!" Olivia said. She stepped daintily into a stall and called out, "We're on our way out. Everybody else has turned in their shoes. They're waiting by the door!"

"Yikes!" Mel cried. "I don't know how I *always* lose track of time!"

She hopped off the bathroom counter and rushed to rejoin her roomies.

Together, they all spilled onto the sidewalk—just in time to catch the very beginning of a thunderstorm.

"Ugh!" Genevieve cried as the raindrops started spattering on the sidewalk. She hopped under an awning next door to Bowlmor. "My hair is toast!"

Olivia looked at her gold watch anxiously. "We have only twenty minutes until our curfew. Shall we get a cab?"

Kiyoko cast a skeptical eye at the sea of yellow cabs whizzing by. Not a one of them had its "available" light lit.

"Trust me," Nick confirmed. "It's not happening. But there's a subway stop nearby. It's a straight shot home on the N/R. Ready to dash?"

Mel didn't even answer. She simply darted out from under the awning and trotted easily across the street.

As she waited for the others at the top of the stairs, she savored the last licks of rain before descending into another New York adventure—the subway.

⟳　　⟳　　⟳　　⟳

Clearly, a few other people had had the same idea. By the time all the interns had bought Metrocards and *chunked* through the turnstiles, the subway platform was milling with damp urbanites, impatient to get home.

After ten minutes of waiting, it also became clear that the trains were *not* running on time.

Nick shook his head good-naturedly.

"Happens every time it rains," he said.

"What happens?" Olivia wondered. She looked like she was trying very hard not to touch anything—or anyone—on the dingy platform.

"The tracks on the F train flooded," Nick said with a shrug, "which means, not only are the trains crowded, our line is delayed."

"We're going to be packed into that train like sardines," Genevieve complained.

But Mel just smiled a secret smile.

Oh, well, she thought mischievously. *If I have to be pressed up against Nick for the duration of our crowded subway ride, so be it.*

⟳　　⟳　　⟳　　⟳

Unfortunately, that scenario had about as much

chance of coming true as the ones Mel had scribbled into her journal. The moment the train finally screeched into the station, the throng of people surged forward en masse. Mel was caught up in the forward motion and hopelessly carried into a subway car.

Just as she passed through its doors, she spotted the rest of her crowd. They were being ferried into the car just next door to hers. They were separated!

As the doors of her car *whooshed* shut, Mel felt momentary panic rise in her throat. But then she reassured herself.

"It's a straight shot home," she heard Nick say in her mind.

Mel looked at the banners that lined the car's ceiling to see how many stops she had to go to get back to the loft.

All she saw was a curve of blank Plexiglass.

Great, Mel thought, *I get the one car with no map! I'll just listen for the announcement.*

Except the next stop came and went *without* any announcement.

Okay, plan C, Mel thought. *Must fight my way to a door and get ready to leap when I see the right street sign.*

Using apologetic smiles, sideways sidles, and, finally, old-fashioned shoving, Mel managed to inch her way to one of the car's doors. And just in time, too! The train was just sliding into her station.

"'Scuse me!" Mel chirped to her fellow passengers.

"Coming through."

Most of them rolled their eyes, but did make grudging motions to let Mel by when the doors opened.

If only the passengers getting *onto* the train could have been so considerate. But before Mel had a chance to hop off the train, they shoved their way *on*, grumbling loudly about the interminable wait they'd endured. Mel was quickly shoved several feet backward. Then she got all turned around in the crowd and lost sight of the doors. By the time she realized what was happening, the doors had closed.

"But—" Mel cried. "No! Wait! That was my stop."

"Okay," she said, sighing to herself. "No biggie. I'll just get off at the next station and double back."

Mel scanned the sea of indifferent people and noticed, finally, a pair of eyes gazing at her. They belonged to a squashy-nosed old man, sitting in a seat nearby, his lap full of newspaper sections.

"Maybe I'll even walk!" she told the man defiantly. "I like the rain anyway."

After a long, beady-eyed silence, the man cracked a grin—which contained a few cracked teeth.

"Ya better like the rain," he said, flipping a page in his folded-up newspaper. "It's a long walk across the Brooklyn Bridge!"

ⓖ　　ⓖ　　ⓖ　　ⓖ

By the time Mel staggered out of the first subway stop in Brooklyn, she was feeling thankful that she'd forgotten to wear her watch. She didn't even want to know how late she was for curfew.

What she *did* want to know was—where could she find a train that would take her back to SoHo?

At first glance, this dark, rain-spattered intersection offered her no clues.

And no people to ask, either.

In fact, the quiet corner felt much farther from bustling Manhattan than a fifteen-minute subway ride. Every storefront Mel looked at was darkened, with a network of bars blocking off its windows. The awnings were rolled up and their illuminated signs had been extinguished.

Occasionally, Mel spotted a shadowy figure— bundled into a raincoat or huddled under an umbrella— dash past across the street. But nobody saw her.

And even if someone had, Mel didn't know if it'd be smart to talk to them.

She suddenly felt more vulnerable and scared than she ever had before. She had a sudden desire to just go home. And not to the loft home. California home.

Mel decided to cross the street and get herself to a more populated area. But the instant she stepped off the curb, she was cut off by a car. She'd been so preoccupied, she almost hadn't seen it.

As the car screeched to a halt, Mel saw that it was

a limo—a shorter one than Jared's superstretch number, but a snazzy ride nonetheless.

Mel bit her lip as one of the car's back windows hummed open. Then she sighed with relief when a young woman poked her head through the window looking alarmed.

"Are you all right?" the girl said. She looked maybe a few years older than Mel. "We almost mowed you down."

"That was my fault," Mel said. "I wasn't paying attention. Bad habit of mine! Listen, do you know where I can get on a subway that'll take me back to Manhattan? I need to get home to SoHo."

"SoHo!" the girl said. "I'm going to Tribeca. Why don't I give you a lift?"

"Um, well . . ." Mel hesitated. Was it safer to get into this car with a stranger? Or to wander the streets of Brooklyn, looking lost?

Mel knew which one was drier. With an impulsive nod, she hopped into the car and told the driver her address. As he pulled away from the curb, the girl gave Mel her business card.

"Minnie Porter-Haywood," she introduced herself. "Just so you know, I'm not some crazy kidnapper."

Mel looked at Minnie's beautiful, open face.

"Okay." She smiled. "I think I can trust you. I'm Mel, by the way. So, you live in Tribeca?"

"Oh noooo," Minnie said. "I was born and raised

on the Upper East Side. I'm *party* hopping in Tribeca. I'm meeting a dozen of my best friends at this loft. Hey, you want to come?"

"Oh," Mel laughed, comparing her own crunchy outfit to Minnie's sleek, red cocktail dress. "I don't think I'd exactly fit in."

"Girlfriend, you're tall, you're blond, you're beautiful," Minnie said frankly. "You'd fit in."

"I'm also only sixteen," Mel admitted with a grin. "I'm just in town for the summer, interning at a magazine."

"Sooooo, maybe you wouldn't fit in!" Minnie admitted with a laugh. "But, ooh, guess what would be perrrrrfect for you?"

"I couldn't even begin to guess," Mel said honestly. She couldn't stop staring at Minnie. With her painted-on dress, her quirky, aristocratic diction, and her confident beauty, she was like someone out of a magazine. She didn't seem quite real.

"*You* should snag yourself a gown and come to this benefit I'm throwing at the end of the month," Minnie declared. "It's to save the manatees. *Such* a good cause!"

"Manatees? I love those," Mel said, even though

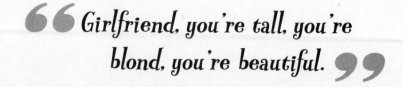

Girlfriend, you're tall, you're blond, you're beautiful.

she had a hard time imagining that Minnie could care that much about the obscure, lumpy mammals. Minnie seemed sweet and all, but an environmentalist? Mel *really* couldn't see that.

"Oh, I can just see you in one of the new Badgley Mischkas at my Manatee Ball," Minnie said blithely. "I could even help you in the makeup department. I'm developing my own line. You know, since Paris is making perfume, I thought I'd try eye shadow. See?"

Minnie closed her eyes to show Mel her snowy, glittery lids.

"It's gonna be called Minnie Me," Minnie went on. "Get it? I think it's totally gonna catch on with the downtown crowd."

"Um, that's really cool!" Mel said, even if she was thinking, *But it's not exactly gonna help us achieve world peace, is it?*

Still, Mel couldn't brush Minnie off as a mere shallow richie. She *had* saved her from the wilds of Brooklyn. For that, Mel gave Minnie a big hug when the chauffeur pulled up in front of her building.

"I totally owe you," Mel said as she climbed out of the limo.

"Then come to the benefit!" Minnie cooed. "Call me, sweetie, and I'll give you the dets."

Mel smiled politely and waved good-bye as the limo pulled away. She had serious doubts that she'd ever make it to Minnie's soiree.

But, oh, what a story I have, Mel thought with a laugh, *to write in my journal*.

Of course, her laughter came to an abrupt halt as she gazed up at the dark windows of her loft.

Feeling her stomach flutter, Mel used her shiny new key to let herself in. She cringed as the elevator landed on her floor with a loud grinding sound. But as she tiptoed across the floor, carrying her noisy flip-flops in her hand, no one stirred.

Except Genevieve, who flipped over in her bed when Mel sneaked into their room. She gave Mel a squint as Mel crept to her bed, peeling off her clothes as she went.

"Well, aren't *you* the party girl," Genevieve said. Her voice was a bit irritated and also a bit admiring. "Have fun breaking curfew? What'd you do out there?"

"I was, um, with Minnie Porter-Haywood," Mel said honestly. She rubbed her eyes. She couldn't wait to hit her pillow.

"Minnie Porter-Haywood?" Genevieve squeaked, sitting up in bed. "Minnie *Porter-Haywood*?"

"Um, yeah?" Mel said as she sleepily set her alarm clock. "Why, do you know her?"

"Who doesn't?" Gen whisper-screamed. "She's only the heiress to the Porter Paper fortune. Y'know, the toilet paper queen?"

Mel's mouth dropped open.

"Minnie just came into her trust fund a few months

❝Do you even read Us Weekly?❞

ago," Gen continued, "and she's been all over the gossip mags ever since. Do you even read *Us Weekly*?"

"No," Mel yawned as she slid beneath her quilt. Her surprise had quickly evaporated. It was replaced by more withering fatigue. "But I promise to tomorrow if you just let me sleep."

Genevieve huffed in frustration. Mel knew she wanted to gossip, but she literally couldn't keep her eyes open a moment longer.

"So don't dish, if you don't want," Genevieve said. Mel heard her flip noisily in her bed. "I just hope you don't oversleep tomorrow. Maybe you can get away with being late to Emma's loft, but at *Flirt*, that's not gonna fly."

Mel's eyes snapped open, and she felt one last zing of worry/panic shoot through her.

Gen's right, she told herself sternly. *Don't oversleep! No oversleeping allowed. The snooze button is verboten. Must get up . . .*

But before she could finish her silent diatribe, her eyelids closed and her mind fuzzed over. Her first day in New York had finally come to a close.

chapter four

And at eight twenty the next morning, her newbie angst promptly returned.

Yes, Mel had set her alarm the night before. However, in her jet-lagged, stressed-out, *completely irresponsible* state, she'd forgotten to turn it on.

Mel stumbled to the side-by-side bathrooms, but both were brimming with her roommates. So she dragged herself to the kitchen, slammed back some coffee, and fished a giant bagel out of a bag on the counter. Then she stumbled back to her room to choose an outfit.

Between the wrinkled gauchos and the wrinkled sundress, Mel decided the sundress was slightly less wrinkled. She laid it out on her bed and—gnawing on her breakfast—went back to the bathrooms.

By the time she wedged herself in at the sink, she was racing with the clock. Quickly, Mel showered, whipped her dirty hair into a couple of buns behind her ears, dashed a bit of tinted moisturizer onto her face, tossed on her dress and a chunky turquoise pendant and her lucky toe ring, and raced out the door after the girls.

Now it was nine o'clock on the dot and Mel was standing outside *Flirt*'s conference room, taking a deep breath.

She tried to smooth down the puckery fabric of her dress,

but when that proved futile, she shrugged.

It's linen, she told herself. *It's supposed to be wrinkly. And besides, it's not like you're gunning for the fashion beat. Writers are all about being rumpled, right?*

From the withering glance Ms. Bishop gave Mel when she stepped through the conference room door, it looked like she was dead, dead wrong.

"Oversleep, did we?" Ms. Bishop said from her chair at the head of the table. She looked as impeccable as

66 *Oversleep, did we?* 99

she had the day before. Arrayed at the table around her, Mel's fellow interns and *Flirt*'s department heads looked almost as good. Genevieve was perfectly prepped out in a houndstooth skirt and short-sleeved sweater. Kiyoko was all about a new-waveish white blouse, and Alexa looked fresh and summery in a raw silk tank. They all wore their glossy, freshly blown hair loose around their shoulders.

"Oh, am I late?" Mel said, glancing at the clock. It was 9:01. That was on time, wasn't it?

Not quite sure how she'd managed to mess up, but quite sure that she *had* messed up, Mel shakily took a seat at the other end of the table. Alexa gave her a sympathetic wink, then turned her attention back to Ms. Bishop. Tension was thick in the air.

"What I am about to tell you, ladies," Bishop announced crisply, "will determine how you spend the rest of your summer. I've decided, based on your applications and my personal assessment of you, which departments you'll be interning with this summer."

Mel caught her breath and glanced at her new friends.

This is it, Mel thought. *Bishop's about to divide and conquer.*

"There are no good or bad assignments here," Ms. Bishop said, giving each of the girls a severe look. "They share equal importance. In each of these departments, you will have the opportunity to distinguish yourselves or to blend in. You can strive for excellence, or merely put in an adequate performance. The choice is yours. I need not tell you what is required to succeed, should you choose to pursue a career in fashion magazines."

Mel felt a shiver travel down her spine. Glancing around the table, she saw that Olivia had gone so pale, she looked almost translucent. Alexa's fingers, cupped beneath her chin, were crossed. And Genevieve looked both defiant and scared.

Every one of them knows which assignment she wants, Mel realized. *Just like me.*

"We'll start," Ms. Bishop announced, breaking into Mel's angst, "with the Health and Fitness section. Charlotte?"

Charlotte squeaked, "Yes?"

"That assignment is yours," Ms. Bishop said imperiously. She turned to Alexa.

"You, Alexa, will be in Photography."

"*Sí, sí, sí!*" Alexa whispered, unable to restrain her giant grin.

"Olivia?"

"Yes, ma'am?"

"Fashion."

At that, Kiyoko went stony faced. She fingered the asymmetrical cuff of her artisan-made blouse and hid her face behind her curtain of hair. Clearly, she'd been hoping for Olivia's beat.

"Kiyoko," Ms. Bishop said, "with your international flair and pop-culture know-how, you're perfect for the Entertainment department."

"Thank you," Kiyoko muttered. Her jaw was tight, Mel noticed, as if she was gritting her teeth.

"And finally, we have Genevieve," Ms. Bishop said, shooting her niece a warm smile. "And Melanie."

No smile for me, Mel noticed miserably.

"Genevieve, your interest in the modeling industry," Ms. Bishop announced, "means you'll be in the Beauty department, one of the magazine's largest."

> **"*No smile for me, Mel noticed miserably.*"**

As Genevieve absorbed this information with a locked jaw of her own, Melanie blinked. And blinked again.

Wait a minute! she realized. *I'm the last one! Which means—*

"And Melanie," Ms. Bishop said, her face twisted

as if she'd just bitten into something sour, "you will be in the Features department. Which means, not only will you be writing articles, but you'll be assisting me with editing, assigning, and other editorial duties."

"Oh, thank you, Ms. Bishop," Mel burst out, knowing her face was shiny with excitement. "You won't be sorry. In fact, I already have a pitch for you! I've been mulling this story for a while and I think it'd be perfect for *Flirt*. It's about teenage girls who are being forced to drop out of their high schools if they get pregnant. It's got everything. Human rights. Women's rights. Teen pregnancy issues! Hot-button-o-rama. It could really make a difference."

Mel's gush of enthusiasm was followed by what could only be called an awkward silence.

O-kay, Mel thought with a shudder. *I guess that means Bishop likes my idea about as much as she likes my outfit.*

"I expect you to go settle in at your work stations," Bishop continued. "In your e-mail accounts, you'll find a dispatch from Delia outlining your first assignments, and the many other duties you'll have as *Flirt* interns. You have only eight weeks here. I hope you'll make them count."

With a chilly smile, Ms. Bishop got to her feet and skimmed out of the conference room. The interns glanced at each other warily.

They were still in this together, but they were no

longer all the same. They'd been divided, all right.

But only some of us have been conquered, Mel thought, glancing at Kiyoko's crestfallen face with a cringe.

Kiyoko, meanwhile, was giving Olivia a sidelong glance.

"Well, I suppose the best girl won," she said bitterly. "Clearly, you've been *living* at the Milan and Paris shows. I've only been to Milan three times and Paris twice."

"Actually," Olivia said with a shrug, "I've never been to Milan. Paris, yes. A few times. Although one of those doesn't count, really. I was only seven at the time."

Alexa laughed, but Kiyoko glowered.

"You've never been to Milan," Kiyoko said bluntly. "But *you* got the Fashion beat while I'm stuck with music and movies. Maybe Bishop thinks I'll have the inside scoop on Puffy AmiYumi or something. Or maybe she just decided to give the gig *I* wanted to her best friend's daughter!"

"Kiyoko!" Olivia gasped. "I'm sorry if you're disappointed. I . . . I thought you'd be happy. I mean, don't you need ten iPods just to keep track of your album collection? You're obsessed with music."

Kiyoko didn't seem at all consoled. She lurched out of her chair and stalked out of the conference room without another word.

The rest of the girls trailed after her and headed

across the cube farm to their cluster of desks. Right behind Mel, Charlotte was whimpering to Genevieve.

"Health and Fitness!" she complained. "That's so lame! You don't think I'm going to have to try out different fitness regimens, do you?

"Whatever," Genevieve snapped. "Health and Fitness is fine, Charlotte. I mean, it's not Beauty, but . . ."

"Wait," Charlotte said, "I thought you wanted Features."

"Oh, please," Genevieve scoffed. Mel winced. Genevieve couldn't have been more than two feet behind her. "Hello? This is *Flirt*! Nobody reads this magazine for the articles. They want to know how to look fabulous. And you can't do that without reading the beauty pages. If you want to get anywhere in magazines, you need to work in Beauty. Or at least Fashion."

"But, you just said," Charlotte protested, "Health and Fitness was fine."

Genevieve just huffed in annoyance. They'd reached their desks by now. On each desk was a computer, a Rolodex, and a nameplate for each intern. Mel's desk was on the corner, just in front of Kiyoko's and next to Charlotte's.

But on Mel's desk was one more thing—a stickie

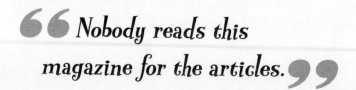

66 Nobody reads this magazine for the articles. 99

affixed to her computer screen that read, *Melanie. Please come to Ms. Bishop's office immediately. Delia.*

She must have liked my idea! Mel realized. *She may not like* me, *but she liked my idea enough to want to talk to me about it. Immediately!*

Mel almost ran through the crowded cube farm to the hallway that led to Ms. Bishop's office. She only paused when she reached an open door next to an austere silver plaque that read *Josephine Bishop, Editor-in-Chief.*

Then she gaped.

While the rest of the *Flirt* office was disheveled and ordinary—filled with average putty-colored furniture, coffee mugs, and office supplies—the anteroom to Bishop's office looked like a movie set. A movie set depicting the office of an ice princess.

Everything—from the shag rug on the bleached-wood floorboards, to the desk at which Delia sat, to the door leading to Bishop's office—was icy white. Mel was almost afraid to step through the door for fear of getting a dirt smudge on one of the gleaming white surfaces.

Alas, she had no choice. From her desk just outside of Bishop's door, Delia spotted Mel lurking.

"Come in, Melanie," she said crisply. "Ms. Bishop is ready to see you."

"Um," Mel said. Feeling more nervous than ever, she rapped on Bishop's door.

"Come in."

Bishop's voice was as sharp as a paper cut. Feeling

her relaxation disappear, Mel opened the door.

Bishop's office was just as white as the anteroom, but it was three times the size. It was outfitted with several shag rugs, a mirrored bar, a giant desk, and a lounge area stocked with brown-and-white cowhide chairs and couches. Mel cringed at the non-vegetarian furniture and was grateful when Ms. Bishop didn't offer her a seat on one.

In fact, she didn't offer Mel a seat at all. Instead, she stood up, walked around her desk, and looked Mel up and down. While Mel squirmed under the scrutiny, Bishop crossed her arms over her chest and pursed her lips.

"Melanie," she said. "I've brought you here to talk about—"

"My story idea?" Mel cut in with a grin.

Bishop gazed at Mel coldly for a moment.

"It's good that you want to hit the ground running," she finally said. "But you are an intern, Melanie. You will accept assignments from me, *not* the other way around. I will give you an assignment that I think you can handle"—Ms. Bishop pressed on—"when I think you're ready."

"Um, okay," Mel said. She'd never met an adult who thought having initiative was a *bad* thing, but then again, she'd never worked at a New York fashion magazine before.

"And you are not ready to be sent out on assignment, to represent *Flirt* magazine," Bishop continued, "until you've done something about this look of yours."

Just as she had in the conference room, Bishop eyed Mel's twin hair buns, her wrinkly outfit, and her flip-flopped feet with distaste. Then she spun on her spike heel and returned to her desk chair. As she sat down, she said, "I want you to go to The Closet. Your first assignment is to compile a wardrobe more befitting an employee at *Flirt*."

With that, Bishop picked up an elegant white pen and began scribbling something on a notepad. She scratched away for a full minute before Mel realized that this was Bishop's way of dismissing her.

"Thank you," Mel murmured before slinking out the door. She shut it behind her and leaned back against it, breathing hard. Out of the corner of her eye, she saw Delia looking at her.

"How'd it go?" she asked cheerily.

"Honestly?" Mel groaned. "I don't know. Bad, I think. Ms. Bishop wants me to go to The Closet."

"I'm not surprised," she said, her perfect eyebrows arched high. She pointed out into the hallway. "It's at the end of the corridor."

"Okay," Mel said shakily.

As a little kid, Mel had never been the type to be scared of the dark. She'd been as unafraid of bogeymen under the bed as she was of the high dive at the pool or being the new kid at school.

And now look at me, Mel thought, leaving the office

on rubbery legs. *I'm sixteen and I'm terrified of a monster in The Closet!*

ⓖ   ⓖ   ⓖ   ⓖ

By the time Mel made it back to the interns' corner, all five of the other girls were clicking away at their computers. Mel tiptoed up to Olivia and tapped her on the shoulder. Olivia jumped.

"Oh. Hi, Mel," she said. "Have you logged in to your system yet? We've all got e-mails from Delia with mile-long to-do lists! I'm going to be running ragged all week!"

But from the pinkness in Olivia's cheeks and the glint in her clear blue eyes, Mel could tell Olivia was loving her first hours at *Flirt.*

Must be nice, she thought wistfully.

"Well, I've just gotten the first item on *my* list," Mel said miserably. "I have to go to The Closet."

Olivia gasped.

"Is it that bad?" Mel wailed. "I don't know what this Closet is! All I know is it has something to do with clothes. And since you're the fashion babe, I was wondering if you could help me."

Before Olivia could reply, Kiyoko had spun around in her chair.

"You're going to The Closet!" she almost screamed. "How'd you get so lucky?"

66 You're going to The Closet! How'd you get so lucky? 99

"But . . . I think this is actually a punishment," Mel protested.

"As if!" Kiyoko declared, springing to her feet. "The Closet is *only* the room where every fashion magazine keeps its treasures—all the clothes, accessories, makeup, and shoes that have been used in every recent photo shoot. *Or* the stuff that's reserved for future shoots. It's like . . . like paradise! That is, *if* you're into fashion."

Kiyoko shot Olivia a snippy look.

"Okay," Mel sputtered, "clearly I'm not so into fashion. But I'm also the one who's got to go assemble some outfits. You guys! I'm desperate! Help!"

"I'm going with you," Olivia assured her.

"Me too!" Kiyoko declared.

"Hey, the more the merrier," Mel said as Olivia and Kiyoko shot scathing looks at each other. "But let's go now!"

ⓖ ⓖ ⓖ ⓖ

"It's . . . it's so much bigger than I'd imagined," Kiyoko choked.

"And so much better!" Olivia breathed.

"Nice to see you agreeing on something," Mel said

drily. "Now can I get a peek?"

Olivia and Kiyoko moved aside to let Mel in. Mel blinked hard and shook her head.

The Closet was more like a warehouse—a warehouse lined with rolling racks of clothes in colors from sunflower to salmon, from gray-black to off-black to black-black. The clothes were crammed in so tight, they looked like pressed flowers.

And little did they know, the clothing racks were hiding more than designer duds. Suddenly the clothes began rustling.

Then a single long leg clad in gray snakeskin pants and a pointy-toed turquoise loafer emerged from the sea of fabric.

Finally the man to whom the leg belonged emerged in full. In his slender-fingered hands, he clutched two gorgeous saffron dresses fluttering from padded hangers. He threw back his head—which was all spiky blond hair, perfectly angled jaw, and carefully kohled blue eyes—and whooped.

"I have come back from the hunt, triumphant!" he cried in a nasal voice that sounded eerily familiar to Melanie. "I am such a big, burly man right now, I think I have a big ol' crush on *myself*!"

He grinned at the three interns, clearly unfazed by the fact that they were perfect strangers, and wafted the dresses in their direction.

"Is that—?" Kiyoko stuttered.

"Indeed it is, Miss Thang," the man said. "Vintage Lagerfeld! These two frocks are from the Poppies line he did in his last year with Chloé. You're beholding rare jewels, girls! Revere!"

Obediently, Kiyoko and Olivia gaped at the gorgeous dresses. But Mel was too busy staring at the man's face.

"Wait a minute!" she said. "Aren't you Jonah Jones? You were at last year's Oscars. You did all that snarky commentary about the stars' outfits. You were the one who made Jennifer Aniston cry when you insulted her dress."

"That is *moi*!" Jonah said proudly.

"I thought you were too busy reading *The New Yorker* to keep up with H-wood gossip," Kiyoko muttered to Mel with a grin.

"Hello?" Mel responded. "I read about it in Talk of the Town. Jonah's the bomb! I even hear his commentary on E! sometimes—when I watch it."

"And you didn't know I worked at *Flirt*?" Jonah scolded Mel. "*Tsk, tsk.* For tonight's homework, little intern, I want you to read the past six issues of *People*, *InStyle*, and *W*."

"How'd you know we were interns?" Melanie said, her eyes wide.

"Who else would come to work dressed like that?" Jonah said, pointing at Mel's outfit in mock horror. "Besides, as you'll learn, Jonah knows all. He sees all.

> **"As you'll learn, Jonah knows all. He sees all. And he's pretty, to boot."**

And he's pretty, to boot. Now *you* must be that California girl I've heard about. Melanie?"

"Yeah!" Mel said, stunned that Jonah knew who she was. "This is Kiyoko and Olivia."

"Obviously!" Jonah said. "Euro-kisses all around, girlfriends. We're gonna have a great summer together."

Jonah fluttered from intern to intern, kissing the air near their cheeks.

"Now, let me plant these little Poppies somewhere safe," Jonah said, hustling his dresses over to a locked cabinet in The Closet's corner. "You see, otherwise *Kristee* would steal them out from under me."

Without missing a beat, Jonah secreted away the Poppies, turned to Mel, Olivia, and Kiyoko, and clapped his hands.

"My name is Jonah and I'll be your tour guide," he announced, gesturing with two fingers like a flight attendant. "Let's look around, shall we?"

Jonah stalked down a narrow aisle next to the clothing racks.

"You've seen the clothes," he announced. "We've got it all here. Stella, Calvin, Miuccia, Donatella . . . We're the best of friends. We feature their frocks in our magazine—and they advertise with us. It's one big back-scratch over here, and we *all* benefit! Now ladies, I have a question for you. What's a frock without the proper . . ."

Having reached the end of the aisle, Jonah paused for dramatic effect, then swung his arm out with a flourish.

". . . shoes?"

Kiyoko and Olivia, and even Mel, gasped as they followed Jonah's gaze.

They were staring at an entire wall of shoes, arranged like jewels in floor to ceiling nooks. They were almost all high heeled. They were strappy and sexy. There were thigh-high boots, cunning anklets, and elegantly simple black pumps. They were amazing.

Once the girls had ogled—and tried on—several pairs of Jimmy Choos and Manolo Blahniks, Jonah led them to a boundless collection of baubles. The real stuff was under lock and key, but the faux necklaces, bracelets, and earrings were there for the taking. Which Kiyoko freely did.

"Ooh," she cried, slipping a giant pink faux diamond onto her ring finger. "Very Nicole Richie."

Beyond the jewelry were bags and belts. Tiny, jeweled clutches, cavernous Kate Spades, and a little pistachio green Marc Jacobs number that made Olivia squeal.

"I've been looking for this for six months!" she cried. "They're on a waiting list."

"Well, keep waiting, dear," Jonah declared,

plucking the bag out of her hands. "That color is so over. Now if we can find it in acid yellow . . ."

Next were scarves and hair accessories, including a few bobby pins with tiny silk flowers on their tips that Jonah scooped up with a mischievous cackle. While Kiyoko and Olivia wandered on to the bank of lipsticks, blushes, foundations, and eye shadows, Jonah grabbed Mel's shoulders and plunked her onto a short stool in front of a wall mirror.

"I can't stand it a minute longer," he cried, pulling Mel's twin hair buns out of their rubber bands. "Sweetie, if you want to call yourself Heidi and go milk a goat on a mountain somewhere, you're allowed to do this with your hair. Otherwise? Not so much."

Finger combing her long waves out, Jonah expertly caught up sections of the hair around Mel's face.

"I'm a genius." He wrapped them into little twists, popped in the pretty bobby pins to hold them in place, and within three minutes, he was done. He fanned his hands around Mel's head.

"I'm a genius," he said.

Mel blinked. The way Jonah had softly pulled her hair off her face made her cheekbones look sharper, her eyebrows archier, and her blue eyes bigger. Meanwhile, the cascade of blond waves around her shoulders looked romantic and neatly professional all at once.

Without waiting for a response, Jonah swept out

> **Sweetie, if you want to call yourself Heidi and go milk a goat on a mountain somewhere, you're allowed to do this with your hair. Otherwise? Not so much.**

of The Closet. The interns dissolved into stunned giggles as they watched him go. But as soon as they regained their composure, their edginess returned. Mel was still in need of an outfit. And Olivia and Kiyoko were still irked with each other.

With one slanted glance at the other, they turned on their heels and headed to opposite sides of The Closet's bank of clothes.

Within a few minutes, Olivia approached Mel with a small stack of clothes.

"You should definitely stock up on some basic classics," she declared, showing Mel a little black dress and a couple of gorgeous silk blouses.

"Are you kidding?" Kiyoko called out from somewhere in the clothes racks. "Mel needs to distinguish herself. And *that* means being fashion-forward."

She fought her way out of the crowded clothing area, clutching some orange bootleg pants, a glitter-trimmed, scoop-necked top, and a dramatic, hand-painted skirt.

"They all look cool to me," Mel shrugged.

Kiyoko and Olivia shot more daggers at each other with their eyes, huffed in frustration, and plunged *back* into the clothing racks.

Olivia returned first.

"Try this on!" she declared, handing a cute little pink suit at Mel. "It's a Chanel, but it's only twenty five hundred American. So you wouldn't have to be nervous about staining it or anything."

"What!?" Mel squeaked.

"Chanel, Shmanel," Kiyoko scoffed, appearing at Mel's side with a skirt of fluttery emerald panels and a one-shouldered, gold tank top. This is much more you, don't you think?"

"But is it Josephine Bishop?" Olivia asked archly.

Kiyoko pressed her lips together in frustration. And then both of the girls dove into their clothes selection *again*.

After twenty more minutes of brutal, competitive dressing, Mel found herself with a new outfit. The rose, A-line skirt and scoop-necked silk top went perfectly with her flowery hairdo. And if the prim, kitten-heeled pumps felt tight and funny on Mel's feet, they *did* look very Josephine Bishop.

Her friends had even made a list of other outfits they thought Mel should snag from The Closet later in the week.

"You'll just stop by every morning," Olivia said with a gleam in her eye, "return the previous day's outfit, and pick up a new one. It's like a dream come true!"

"For you!" Mel laughed. But she couldn't help sneaking glances at herself in the full-length mirror next to The Closet's door. She looked very *Flirt*.

Well, if I haven't spent the second morning of my internship doing serious journalism, she told herself, *I have had some fun!*

And now, Mel thought hopefully as she and her friends headed back to their desks, *let's just hope Bishop lets me do what I'm actually* supposed *to—write some killer copy for* Flirt!

chapter five

Okay, when I said I wanted to write some killer copy, I didn't mean it literally!

It was Mel's third morning at *Flirt* and she was staring in horror at the e-mail on her computer screen. It was her first feature assignment from Bishop.

The Florent Company, Bishop had written, *is about to launch a new perfume called Thoughtful. This prompts the question—what goes into the creation of a major new scent? It will be your job, Melanie, to tell us. I want you to do a behind-the-scenes look at the perfume division of the Florent Company. You are to interview the vice president of the perfume division, tour the laboratory, work as a "nose" who mixes scents, and then write a scintillating fifteen-hundred-word article about it all. I've attached contact names and phone numbers (and wardrobe suggestions) below.*

After that, the text on the computer screen got blurry.

The Florent Company? Mel squawked in her head. *The Florent Company is only the most evil cosmetic manufacturer around! I know that most of the cosmetics companies use animal testing. I mean, if they don't say they* don't, *it means they probably do. But at least they try to be hush-hush about it. The Florent Company, on the other hand, is so unapologetic about their animal torture, they practically advertise it! PETA staged a major protest against Florent last year and everyone at my school has been boycotting them for years! Can Bishop not know how evil they are?*

Bishop is totally insulated from the real world in there, Mel complained to herself. *Which means . . .*

Mel cocked her head and her eyes widened.

Hey! Maybe she really doesn't *know about how evil Florent is. As a reporter, isn't it my duty to tell her?*

Jumping out of her chair, Mel marched to Bishop's office.

When she arrived, Delia's desk was empty.

Mel hesitated only a moment before deciding that she didn't have to wait for Delia's return. She'd go ahead and knock on Bishop's half-open door herself.

The only glitch in the plan?

Somebody was already in Bishop's office.

"Aunt Jo, you know I think the Beauty beat is amazing, but don't you think I could make more of a contribution in Features? I'm just thinking about the good of the magazine . . ."

Mel's mouth dropped open. The voice clearly belonged to Genevieve. And Genevieve was clearly trying to use her family connections to get Melanie's gig.

". . . Plus, if I were to do some modeling for the magazine," Genevieve added, "I could learn so much about beauty there. It would kill two birds with one stone!"

Whoa! Mel thought, reeling. *And I thought* I *had chutzpah. Gen's lucky she's Bishop's niece. I could never get away with a proposition like that!*

"Genevieve," Ms. Bishop said. "In case you've forgotten, I'm thinking of the good of the magazine, too. That is precisely why I gave you the Beauty internship. That is where I think you serve *Flirt* best."

"But—"

"Besides," Bishop went on, "you love this subject. Remember when we went to Bergdorf's a few months ago? You were able to tell me the name of every color in Chanel's new lip gloss line. And you practically delivered a thesis on the history of M.A.C. It was then and there that I decided that Beauty would be the beat for you."

"Oh . . ." Genevieve said quietly. Mel could plainly hear the regret in her voice. She was kind of surprised that Bishop couldn't.

Maybe I was wrong, she realized. *Maybe even Genevieve can't get a break from Bishop.*

"Well," Gen wheedled, "what about—"

Again, Bishop couldn't be bothered to wait for Genevieve's question.

"As for the modeling," she announced, "Genevieve, you're a perfectly attractive girl. You do an excellent job using makeup to highlight your best features. But you know very well that you're too short for editorial or runway work. Maybe you could try catalogs some day, but really, I think you'd be much better served spending your internship focusing on your writing."

Mel cringed.

Harshola, she thought.

Apparently, Genevieve agreed, because a quick moment later, she appeared in Bishop's door, her eyes glittering and her mouth pressed into a tight line. When she spotted Mel fidgeting next to Delia's still-empty desk, her eyes went wide. She stared at Mel in shock.

Mel didn't want to say anything, just in case Bishop's ears were as sharp as her tongue. So she merely gave Genevieve a sympathetic smile.

To which Genevieve responded with a sneer.

"I was just making a shopping date with my aunt," she told Mel breezily, blinking her tears away. "It's a thing with us. We're *very* close."

"That sounds . . . nice?" Mel said. She was too occupied with her own agenda to deal anyway. As Genevieve flounced out of the anteroom with a toss of her curly hair, Mel sidled up to Bishop's door and knocked on it softly.

"Um . . . Ms. Bishop?"

ⓖ   ⓖ   ⓖ   ⓖ

Liv_B-C: What happened?

Mel_H: Bishop interface—ugh.

Liv_B-C: You were called in
for another meeting? But

you look so great, Mel!

Mel_H: It wasn't the look. I assume
my outfit passed, since Bishop
didn't mention it. No, I went
in voluntarily. She wants me 2
write a piece of PROPAGANDA about
this cruel cosmetic company.

Liv_B-C: Cruel? Oh, like those
lip plumpers that sting?

Mel_H: As in cruel to animals!
Which I assumed Bishop didn't
know. Else why would she want
me 2 write about Florent?

Liv_B-C: Sure. What did she say?

Mel_H: For all I know, she didn't
hear a word I said. She never even
looked up from the notebook she was
writing in. She just said something
about me having 2 be a team player if
I ever wanted to make it in NY mags.

Liv_B-C: I guess that's, like,
office speak?

Mel_H: Well I'M guessing I still have to do this story. I can't believe this. My integrity as a journalist is shot, right out of the gate.

Liv_B-C: Isn't there some way you could—

Before Mel could finish reading Olivia's message, Genevieve popped up next to her desk, smiling widely. Clearly, she'd gotten over whatever Bishop damage she'd been sporting a few minutes earlier.

"I don't know about you," she sighed, "but this office scene is a drag. Want to go on a Creami D-Lite run?"

Mel glanced at her computer screen. In addition to stonewalling her in her office, Bishop had reminded Mel that she had only a week to turn in a first draft of her Florent story. Mel had to get started, no matter how much she dreaded it.

Then again, Mel thought, *maybe it'd be a good idea to clear my head, and ingest some sugar, before I start.*

"Sure," she said with a shrug.

Instantly, Olivia was at Mel's side, shooting Genevieve a suspicious look.

"I'll go too!" Olivia announced. "Creami D-Lite's that low-fat ice cream, eh? Yum!"

"Whatev," Genevieve said. She began stalking

away, which gave Olivia the opportunity to grab Mel's elbow.

"Are you sure it's a good idea?" she whispered. "Hanging out with Genevieve?"

"Sure, why not?" Mel shrugged. "Maybe some ice cream will mellow her out!"

"Well, just in case it doesn't," Olivia whispered, "I want to be there to protect you!"

"Liv!" Mel laughed. "You act like we're going to war or something!"

"Maybe we are," Olivia said, frowning at Genevieve's stiff back.

"So," Genevieve said carefully as the girls reached the *Flirt* vestibule and stepped into an elevator, "what was that all about? Your meeting with my aunt?"

Mel vaguely noticed Olivia's eyes widening with alarm, but she had no problem answering. In fact, now that she'd heard how Bishop had treated her niece, Mel sort of felt like she had an ally in Genevieve.

"Oh, I guess you could call it a difference of opinion," Mel said. "About the Florent Company."

"Really?" Genevieve said. She was all interest as the girls crossed the lobby and emerged onto the street.

"Now that she'd heard how Bishop had treated her niece, Mel sort of felt like she had an ally in Genevieve."

> **So, how do they make Creami D-Lite so low cal?**

"Does she want you to write something about them?"

"So, how do they make Creami D-Lite so low cal?" Olivia blurted. "Is it yogurt or something?"

Olivia's ploy didn't work. Genevieve ignored her and continued talking to Mel.

"I take it," she said loudly, "you don't want to write about Florent because of their animal-testing rep?"

"How did you know?" Mel asked, wondering if Genevieve had eavesdropped on *her* conversation with Bishop, too.

"Oh, please," Genevieve scoffed. "Everyone knows that Florent is public enemy number one for crunchy Cali types like you."

"Dude," Mel said. "Have you seen what they do to rabbits? They stick mascara *in their eyes*."

"Oh yeah, it's horrible," Genevieve said, sounding bored. Then she paused before a tiny hole-in-the-wall storefront. It seemed to be overflowing with tall, skinny women in outfits that looked a lot like Mel's.

"Creami D is quite the Hudson-Bennett hang," Genevieve said knowingly. The girls went inside to regard the bank of soft-serve ice-cream machines and the list of that day's flavors.

"Peanut Butter Fudge," Olivia read. "Blueberry

Cheesecake. Crème Brûlée? Cake Batter? Ick. All we have in London is chocolate and vanilla."

"Welcome to America," Mel joked. "Inventor of the freeze-dried french fry and *anything* artificially flavored. Not that I've ever had this stuff. I'm all about real ice cream. Ben and Jerry are my best buds!"

Genevieve stopped perusing the calorie chart on the counter to turn and gape at Mel.

"How do you stay so skinny?" she demanded angrily.

"I don't know," Mel shrugged. "I'm kinda hyper, I guess."

Rolling her eyes again, Genevieve muttered, "It must be nice to always have things go your way. You almost kill a pizza guy on a scooter, and he calls you beautiful. You show up at *Flirt* looking like Princess Leia after an all-night rave, and you get the Features internship. You eat nothing but cream puffs and ice cream, and you have, like, two percent body fat."

"Oh," Mel said sheepishly, "you're totally exaggerating, Gen."

Genevieve shrugged with exaggerated indifference, then turned to order a small cup of Coffee Toffee. Olivia went for Toasted Coconut.

"I'll have Chocolate Marshmallow," Mel told the guy behind the counter. "Ooh, can I have that in a waffle cone? With some sprinkles?"

Genevieve grumbled some more, especially when

Mel took her first bite of Creami D-Lite.

"It's kind of air-puffed, isn't it?" she said, rolling the odd confection around in her mouth.

"That's because it's low cal," Genevieve remarked, slowly licking her ice cream off her spoon. "You know," she continued, "if you really hate the Florent story that much, you shouldn't do it."

"*What?*" Mel and Olivia said together.

"Well, I don't mean you shouldn't write *a* story," Genevieve said. "Please. Aunt Jo would kill you. What I mean is—if you just regurgitate exactly what Aunt Jo wants, she's gonna think that's all you're capable of. She'll think you're just a yes-girl. Not a real journalist."

"Omigod," Mel said. "That's just what I was thinking when I went to her office! But from all the signals she sent me, I think she *does* want a yes-girl. She says I'm not ready to make my own assignments."

"Well," Olivia cautioned, "if that's what she said, then—"

"Believe me," Genevieve interrupted. "I know my Aunt Jo. Sure, she *says* she doesn't want people to rock the boat. If everyone at *Flirt* did that, it would be anarchy! But listen, Mel. You only have eight weeks to

If you have a chance to give Aunt Jo bigger and better than what she expects of you, you'd be a fool to pass it up.

prove yourself here. If you have a chance to give Aunt Jo bigger and better than what she expects of you, you'd be a fool to pass it up."

"Really?" Mel said, taking an eager bite of her Creami D-Lite and grimacing through its puffy texture. "That's what I was thinking, too!"

"Mel," Olivia said warily, "I really don't know if that's such a good idea."

"Listen," Genevieve said dismissively. "Josephine Bishop is my aunt. I think I know her a little better than you. And I'm only trying to give Mel a little help. You know, since she got off on such a bad foot at *Flirt*."

Mel cringed, but she couldn't deny that Genevieve was right.

"Maybe," Mel said, her bad mood beginning to lift already, "my mistake was in pitching my story to Bishop. Asking for permission to do my own thing isn't really doing my own thing, is it? If I just forge ahead and kick butt while I'm at it, that'll *really* prove to Bishop that I'm journalist material."

"But Mel," Olivia pointed out, "Ms. Bishop didn't really seem to fancy your story idea about teen pregnancy. Don't you think she'd be even more mad if you went for it anyway?"

"Totally!" Mel said cheerfully. "That's why I have to come up with something else. Something fabulous."

"You go, girlfriend," Genevieve said, pumping her fist before scraping her last bite of Creami D-Lite out of her cup. Genevieve's encouragement, Mel had to admit, sounded a little wooden, but she thought it was nice of Genevieve to try.

"Thanks, sweetie!" Mel said, throwing her free arm around Genevieve's shoulders and giving her a squeeze. "You've totally pulled me out of my Florent funk! Though I gotta say, this Creami D-Lite stuff? It *so* pales next to Marsha Marsha Marshmallow."

Sticking out her tongue and laughing, Mel lobbed her half-eaten cone at a nearby garbage can.

Although, as she and her friends strode back into the Hudson-Bennett building, she realized that maybe the snack had worked after all. Now that she'd decided to do her own article for Bishop, she felt ready to seriously get to work dreaming up the new idea.

Like Genevieve said, Mel thought, *things seem to go my way. With any luck, Bishop will go my way, too!*

chapter six

That evening, Mel was kicking back on the couch reading when Kiyoko shuffled into the living area of the loft bearing menus and a determined expression.

"I'm thinking sushi," she said. "What do you guys say?"

"Mmm, sushi takeout?" Mel piped up. "Sounds delish."

"Actually," Alexa said, coming down the stairs and pulling her freshly brushed hair into a loosely stylish topknot, "why don't we go out? There's still a lot of New York to experience, you know!"

Mel hesitated. She'd sort of been planning on spending the evening at home, doing some Googling to try to come up with a non-Florent story idea.

On the other hand, Mel thought, eyeing Nick in his completely cute (and sorta tight) T-shirt, *it has been a really long day. And I can always go for some veggie rolls . . .*

"You're right!" Mel declared. "Let's go out!"

"Why don't you guys try Tomoe?" Nick piped up. He'd been leaning against the kitchen counter, guzzling some iced tea while the girls talked. "It's this tiny place in the West Village. There's no atmosphere whatsoever, but it's the *best* sushi downtown.

People have been known to stand in line for hours to get in."

After exchanging a quick nod with her buds, Mel exclaimed, "Let's do it! Where is this Tomoe?"

"Well, it's on Thompson Street," Nick began, "between—"

"I have a better idea," Mel interrupted with a grin. "Why don't you join us for dinner? Then you can just show us where it is."

"Yes, that'll be fun!" Olivia said.

"And I'll grab Genevieve and Charlotte," Mel said, heading across the loft. "I think they're camped out in our room."

While I'm in there, Mel thought, *I'll put on one of the cute new outfits Jonah gave me from The Closet the other day! Six girls and one guy doesn't exactly make for a traditional date, but hey, I'll take it!*

When Mel emerged from her bedroom five minutes later, though, she was distressed to see that Nick had disappeared.

"Um, what happened to Nick?" Mel wondered, trying to sound casual.

"He said he'd love to come," Alexa shrugged, "but he had other plans. Don't worry, though. He wrote down directions to Tomoe for us. We can walk there!"

"Huzzah!" Olivia cried. "No subways."

"Huzzah," Mel echoed, trying to keep the disappointment out of her voice.

But apparently, it didn't work. Kiyoko shot her a curious squint.

"Oh, I get it!" she said suddenly. "Mel, you're totally in like with Nick!"

"What!" Mel cried.

"What?" Genevieve huffed, giving Mel a sudden glare.

"Look at you!" Kiyoko went on. "That filmy tank top and those skinny black pants are totally a date outfit! You've even got some pink sparkly stuff on your cheeks. You're crushing. It's so cute!"

"Wellll," Mel said. She hesitated for only an instant before she broke. "Okay, it's true," she blurted. "I like Nick soooo much. I mean, he's so sweet. And he's so good-looking. And he—"

"—seemed really sorry he couldn't come to dinner." Alexa interrupted. "Mel, maybe he likes you, too!"

"I don't know," Genevieve said, a sour look on her face. "Nick and I are pretty friendly. Y'know, I lived here when I was an intern last summer, too, and we got to know each other. But he hasn't asked me about you at all, Mel."

"Oooh." Mel's excitement had quickly deflated.

"That doesn't mean anything," Olivia piped up. "The last thing any savvy boy would do was ask her *roommate* about the girl he fancied. That's as good as parking himself under her balcony and serenading her.

66 *It smells better downtown.* 99

The bloke has to play it cool, at least at first."

"Good point!" Mel said, perking up. She smiled at her buds gratefully. "And you know what else? Much as I dig Nick, I'm not *that* disappointed that he's not joining us tonight. We'll have a girls' night! It'll be great."

6　　6　　6　　6

Mel breathed deeply as the girls wended their way through the streets of SoHo.

"It smells better downtown," she decided. "Midtown is so smoggy, isn't it?"

She sighed as the girls reached a corner on a busy avenue. A few steps away, she spotted a newsstand on the curb. Impulsively, Mel ran over to it. As the girls followed, she grabbed a copy of *Flirt* and flipped to the masthead at the front of the issue. JOSEPHINE BISHOP—EDITOR-IN-CHIEF topped the masthead in bold print.

Beneath that were her friends' bosses, Lynn Stein, Demetria Tish, Trey Narkisian, and plenty of other names that were slowly becoming familiar to Mel. Mel showed the page to her friends.

"Can you believe," she burbled, "that *our* names are going to be on this masthead? 'Interns, Charlotte Gabel, Alexa Veron, Genevieve Bishop, Olivia Bourne-

Cecil, Kiyoko Katsuda—' "

"—and last but not least," Alexa cut in, adopting the booming voice of a TV announcer, "the gorgeous, the destined-to-be-famous, the very-clumsy-on-Rollerblades, Melanie Henderson!"

"Actually," Genevieve said, "on that list of interns, my name will be first."

"Wh-what?" Mel said.

"Well, we'll be listed in alphabetical order, of course," Genevieve pointed out.

"Whatever," she heard Kiyoko mutter.

Olivia, who seemed to have a knack for changing the subject when things got tense, suddenly pointed at a large magazine with a red banner.

"Ooh, *Hello!* magazine," she cooed, grabbing up a copy. "This makes me homesick for London. Let's see what Prince Harry is up to this week . . ."

But Olivia had barely begun to flip through the gossipy mag when, suddenly, she froze and went pale. A moment later, her cheeks turned crimson.

"*¿Que pasa?*" Alexa said, sidling up to Olivia's side. "What is it?"

Gently, Alexa took the *Hello!* from Olivia and gave it a once-over. Then *she* froze.

"Oh," she said. "Oh my."

Kiyoko grabbed the mag and read aloud.

"'Paris art dealer Matthew Bourne-Cecil was recently spotted leaving Harrod's with Emmeline, the renowned fashion model/artist, on his arm. And on *her* arm? A tiny shopping bag that could contain nothing other than jewelry. Unless it was a very small item of lingerie.' "

"It's probably nothing," Olivia said shakily, looking down at her hands. "My parents' gallery represents Emmeline's paintings. Leave it to *Hello!* to be so inflammatory."

She cast a quick, and sympathetic, glance in Olivia's direction. Then she tossed the magazine back onto the newsstand with a disdainful sniff and turned on her heel. "We're outta here."

"Hey," said the guy behind the newsstand, a shaggy-haired man in his twenties. "Don't ya want to buy nothin'?"

Kiyoko glanced back at him, smiled icily, and said, "Later, sweetie." As she and her friends stalked back to the corner, she added, "Sometimes having guys hit on you *everywhere* you go can be a real distraction."

Alexa slapped a hand over her mouth to try to hide her laughter. But when she spotted a storefront on the other side of the street, she took her hand away to squeal. "Now *there's* a distraction! Hey, you guys, let's go in there!"

Mel followed Alexa's gaze to a sign that read *Mehndi Your Way—Henna Tattoos.*

"Ooh, fun!" Mel said.

Alexa hooked her arm through Olivia's.

"C'mon," she urged Olivia. "Don't you want a henna tattoo?"

"Oh, I don't know," Olivia said uncertainly. "That's not very . . . me."

"Not very you?" Kiyoko wondered. "Or not very Bourne-Cecil?"

Mel noticed that, for the first time since Olivia had gotten the fashion internship, Kiyoko had spoken to her in a normal tone of voice, rather than a snipe or a snap.

"Olivia," Kiyoko said softly, "I know what it's like to have parents in the public eye. But you don't *always* have to be on your guard. I mean, if your dad can allow himself to be, um, accidentally caught in an . . . inflammatory photo, I think you can get away with a little tattoo. What's the harm?"

> **I know what it's like to have parents in the public eye. But you don't always have to be on your guard.**

By the time Kiyoko had finished her pep talk, Olivia was smiling.

"You know," she said, "I think you just may be right. What *is* the harm?"

And the next thing Mel knew, Olivia was marching their group across the street to the tattoo shop.

ⓖ   ⓖ   ⓖ   ⓖ

"Ooh!" Alexa squealed a half hour later as the girls emerged from the tattoo parlor. "This stuff tickles when it comes off!"

The mehndi artist who'd "tattooed" her, Mel, Olivia, and Kiyoko had instructed them to let the clay-like henna dry on their skin and flake off as they went about their evening. Underneath the clay, their skin would emerge stained with reddish-brown designs.

Alexa had gotten a spray of vines and a gleaming sun on her sternum, just above her ample cleavage. Kiyoko's tattoo was a bright-eyed manga character, dancing on her skinny bicep. Mel had a daisy-chain choker around her neck. And Olivia, answering Kiyoko's call to rebellion, had had a beautiful twining Indian design painted onto the tops of both her feet.

"How's mine look?" Mel giggled, lifting her chin to give her friends a peek. "It's pretty, isn't it?"

"Not as pretty as my feet!" Olivia laughed, skipping a few steps down the sidewalk. Then she glanced at Genevieve and Charlotte, who weren't nearly as giddy as the other interns. "Hey, how come you guys decided not to get tattoos? It wasn't too expensive, I hope?"

"Of course not," Genevieve said. "It's just, well, my Aunt Jo."

This stopped everyone in their tracks.

"It's no big deal," Genevieve confirmed. "She's just viciously anti-tattoo, that's all. She hates that all the models have them these days. She makes the art director air brush them out of every picture. It probably adds an extra day to production every issue."

Kiyoko planted her fists on her hips so hard, a little spray of henna popped off her upper arm.

"Genevieve," she barked. "You could have told us."

"Yeah," Mel said, feeling totally confused. "Why didn't you?"

"You guys were so excited to get your little tattoos," Charlotte piped up. "Genevieve didn't want to spoil your fun."

"Well, that's nice," Mel said. "I guess. Anyway, this is no biggie, right? I mean, these tats *can* be washed off."

"They fade away," Olivia said miserably. "In one to four weeks! That's what the artist told me."

"Okay," Mel said regretfully, "I guess tomorrow I hit The Closet for a collection of chokers to cover up my daisies."

"And I can kiss all my sandals good-bye for the next month," Olivia complained.

Kiyoko seemed too mad to talk. She just pulled out the directions to Tomoe and began to lead the girls toward it, walking so fast, they almost had to run to keep up with her.

Girls' night had taken a turn for the tense, that was for sure.

On the bright side, the wait for a table at Tomoe was only twenty minutes and the sushi was, indeed, as delectable as Nick had promised. And dirt cheap, too.

But the group's ebullient mood had definitely dampened a bit. Except, that was, where Genevieve was concerned. While she helped herself to as much high-protein, low-fat sashimi as she wanted, she burbled on about some of the other oh-so-hot New York joints the girls should hit that summer.

"Trust me," she told her friends, "living in Connecticut, I come into the city *all* the time."

She clearly loved being in the know about this designer's boutique and that perfect little brunch spot, the piano bar at a certain hotel that didn't mind if you weren't twenty-one, and the warehouse in Gramercy Park that occasionally held the most awesome sample sales.

"Oh, and I almost forgot," Genevieve added at the end of her long monologue, "the Ryan Space."

"What's that?" Olivia asked dully.

"Only one of the hottest galleries in Chelsea," Genevieve said haughtily. She turned to Mel, a sly smile on her face.

"Didn't Nick mention it to you?" Gen asked, her voice dripping with faux sweetness, "during one of your little chats? He told *me* all about it. He's having an opening there on Tuesday! It's a multi-artist show, all abstract painters like Nick. It'll be awesome."

"Oh!" Mel said. Instantly an intense desire bloomed in her belly. She wanted Nick to invite her to his opening.

"You should totally go to the opening," Genevieve told Mel, as if she'd read her mind.

"Well, if Nick asked me to, I would in a heartbeat," Mel said, glancing around at her other roomies. She noticed Alexa and Kiyoko glancing at each other, their eyebrows raised and their mouths turned down in twin frowns.

"I wouldn't expect him to ask," Genevieve said quickly. "Remember, Nick and I are buds. And I can tell you, he's . . . kind of shy. Plus, he might not think it's appropriate to ask you to his show, you being an intern and all."

"Oh, right," Mel nodded. "Hadn't thought of that."

"But I bet he'd be blown away," Genevieve said with a gleam in her eyes, "if you showed up and surprised him!"

"But, Genevieve," Charlotte half-whispered, "what about Nick's g—"

66 *He might not think it's appropriate to ask you to his show, you being an intern and all.* **99**

"Does anyone want that last piece of yellowtail?" Genevieve asked, pointing at a plump piece of fish with her chopsticks—and neatly cutting Charlotte off.

Mel barely heard her. She'd pretty much zoned out after Genevieve had made her proposal. Her *brilliant* proposal.

"Um, Mel?" Olivia said, snapping her fingers in front of Mel's face. Mel blinked hard, aware of her eyes refocusing.

"Whoa, you were really zoned," Alexa laughed. "What were you thinking about, space girl?"

"Oh," Mel covered up, "my article. I'm still trying to figure out what to do. Y'know, pursuing that truth and justice thing? It's kinda hard!"

"Keep plugging, girlfriend," Genevieve encouraged her, taking a slurp of green tea. Then she smiled coldly as she waved her mani'd fingers at a server. "Check, please."

The girls took a meandering walk home, wandering through the streets of the Village, stopping now and then in quaint little bakeries and tiny but fabulous clothing boutiques. While Mel enjoyed chatting with her buds as they soaked in New York, part of her was caught up in daydreams about Nick.

And clearly, her crushy haze was totally obvious, because Kiyoko looped her arm through Mel's and led her down the sidewalk, a couple of storefronts away from their friends.

> **She can't be trusted. I don't know what kind of scheme she's got going, telling you to go to Nick's opening. But I think there definitely _is_ one. Maybe she knows something about Nick we don't.**

"So what do you think of Genevieve's suggestion?" Kiyoko said, pausing for the moment in the light flooding out of a bookshop window.

"To go to Nick's art opening?" Mel said with a grin. "I think it's stellar!"

"Well, I think it's treachery," Kiyoko said darkly. "The girl totally let us get those tattoos on purpose." She pointed to the amber flowers encircling Mel's neck. "She can't be trusted. I don't know what kind of scheme she's got going, telling you to go to Nick's opening. But I think there definitely _is_ one. Maybe she knows something about Nick we don't."

"Don't worry!" Mel assured her. "I have a good feeling about it. I've never felt this way about anyone before, Keeks. I really think Nick is meant to be my boyfriend. My first boyfriend ever. Even if she _does_ want to, Genevieve can't come between us."

chapter seven

The next morning Mel awoke to a mild but persistant sense of panic. She was still racking her brain for a feature idea that would blow Bishop away. She needed something that would both promote cosmetics, thus making Bishop happy, and also have a social consciousness, thus allowing Mel to live with herself.

It was beginning to seem like a tall order.

Breakfast could help, Mel decided. *Maybe I'll go out in search of some hot doughnuts.*

Being careful not to wake Genevieve, who was still asleep with a satin mask over her eyes, Mel slithered out of bed. She pulled on some cotton shorts and a tank top and tiptoed out of the room.

She was surprised to find Alexa up as well. She was multitasking at the kitchen counter—stretching out her quad muscles, sipping at a steamy mug, *and* studying something intensely. When she heard Mel's door open, she glanced up and grinned.

"*Hola,*" she whispered. "I'm just having some *café* before I go out for a run. You wanna come with?"

"Oh," Mel yawned, stumbling up to the counter to join Alexa, "running sounds fun and all, but a nice sticky bear claw sounds even better!"

Alexa laughed and went back to gazing at the piece of paper on the counter. Mel saw that it was a glossy contact sheet—about thirty tiny photos all lined up on one page.

"What're those?" Mel asked, nodding at the colorful little images.

"Oh," Alexa said with a frown, "my first assignment from Bishop. She made me do a bunch of product shots. You know, take a pot of face cream or a lipstick or something, light it artfully, and shoot. Not exactly the kind of portraits I usually like to do."

From beneath the contact sheet, Alexa slid another glossy page. This was a candid shot. In it, a woman sipped from a paper cup and stared out the window. She looked wistful. Though she was draped in black and a bit dowdy, a shaft of sunlight hitting her face made her look downright beatific.

In the blurred background of the shot, Mel spotted a small table draped in a white cloth and stacked with a couple of colorful jars.

"Did you take this picture during the product shoot yesterday?" Mel asked Alexa.

"*Sí,*" Alexa nodded, taking another slurp of coffee.

"I think you should show this pic to Bishop," Mel said. "It rocks. You shouldn't be wasting your time shooting makeup!"

"What, I should talk to Bishop because it worked so well for you?" Alexa sighed, patting Mel's shoulder kindly.

"No, I think I'd better do what she says. It's funny, I never care about cutting up at school. I've gotten so many demerits, I couldn't count them. I was even suspended once for a day."

"What'd you do?" Mel gasped.

"Let's just say," Alexa said with a sly grin, "it involved the brattiest girl in school and some royal blue hair dye."

"Oooh," Mel laughed. "You are bad."

"But this summer's different," Alexa said, her face going earnest. "I mean, I bend the rules a little at school because their rules are so silly. But here? Well, all I want to do is take awesome photos, you know? That's what I want to do with my life, so this is a really big chance for me. Plus, I don't want this to be the last time *Mami y Papi* ever let me out of their sight!"

> ## All I want to do is take awesome photos, you know?

"I hear ya!" Mel giggled. And she really did. She and Alexa had a lot to gain this summer at *Flirt*. But they also had a lot to lose.

But does that have to mean, Mel wondered, *that we just mindlessly accept Bishop's Mickey Mouse assignments without even trying to do them better? What's the right answer?*

Mel gave Alexa another searching look.

I don't know, but maybe together, Alexa and I can figure it out.

"You know what?" Mel said. "I think I will take that run with you after all."

๏   ๏   ๏   ๏

Alexa loped up the West Side Highway looking for all the world like a graceful gazelle, complete with her long, black ponytail streaming out behind her.

Mel, on the other hand, felt more like a gimpy giraffe. Between the stitch in her side and the tightness in her hamstrings, it was all she could do to keep up with Alexa for more than a mile. After that, Mel made a bargain with her. Run four blocks, then walk four blocks, before running again.

During the walking parts, Mel told Alexa about her Bishop dilemma.

"This Florent story is nothing more than an advertorial," she complained between huffs and puffs.

"Just like my product photos," Alexa grumbled.

"But I can't think of an alternative that would wow Bishop enough to make her forgive me for disobeying her," Mel said. "I think Bishop cares about us doing what she says more than anything."

At that, Alexa gasped.

Then she got a mischievous gleam in her eyes.

"That's it!" she cried.

"That's what?" Mel said. She noticed that they were just passing the four-block mark—the point at which they were supposed to start running again. But Alexa was so excited, she didn't even notice.

"You *will* do the Florent story," Alexa exclaimed.

"And that's solving the problem *how*?" Mel said, immediately deflated.

"What did Bishop say she wanted?" Alexa said. "A behind-the-scenes look at the Florent Company, right? So you give her exactly what she asked for."

"The thing is," Mel explained, "she doesn't *really* want that. She wants me to paint this sanitized picture of the place, complete with sound bites from some VP and a 'tour' of the lab where people sit around sniffing stuff."

"Let me repeat my question," Alexa said, looking more gleeful than ever. "Bishop wants a behind-the-scenes look at the Florent Company, riiiiight?"

"Wait a minute," Mel gasped. "You're saying—"

"You *really* go behind the scenes," Alexa proposed.

"To the place where . . . mice are doused with perfume?" Mel said.

"And rabbits are forced to test makeup," Alexa confirmed. "Of course, we'll have to go undercover to get that kind of story."

"*We'll* have to go undercover?" Mel said.

"*Chica*," Alexa proclaimed, "you've got to have

pictures to go with your exposé, do you not?"

"Whoo-hoo!" Mel shrieked, giving Alexa a big, sweaty hug. "I'll give Bishop the story she wants, but I'll do it my way. After that, she'll *have* to be convinced that Florent is an evil company that doesn't deserve to be given a puff piece in *Flirt*!"

"This is the *best* idea," Mel said, grinning at Alexa gratefully. "Not only will Florent get what it deserves—"

"*If* we can dig up the right dirt on them," Alexa qualified.

"—but we'll also prove to Bishop that we're no lightweights," Mel said. "If we succeed, Alexa, we'll spend the rest of the summer doing work that's just as cool as this story."

"I can kiss my studio shots of body butter good-bye!" Alexa shouted triumphantly.

"And I can accomplish what I wanted to this summer," Mel said with a shiver of happiness. "Writing something that makes a difference in the world."

"Hey," Alexa said, finally noticing that the girls were blocks beyond their start-running point, "if we don't run home, we'll probably be late for work."

"Say no more," Mel sighed with a wry smile. The girls turned around and began their gazelle-versus-giraffe race home.

◉   ◉   ◉   ◉

The next morning, Mel popped her head around

The Closet door. "I need a confidence booster," she said. "I'm starting my big feature today. Make me into a hard-nosed journalist, bay-bee!"

"One of those dowdy things?" Jonah protested. "Never! However . . ."

Jonah put a finger to his chin as he pondered for a moment. Then he dove into the crowded clothes rack. Mel had *no* idea how Jonah could find anything in that chaos, but he insisted he had a system.

Mel was inclined to believe him when he emerged in two minutes flat holding the perfect outfit for Mel—an ankle-sweeping black skirt with geometric shapes cut out of the bottom half to lighten it up. And on top, a cap-sleeved white blouse with a cute peplum and buttons that looked like red daisies. Finally, there was a black ribbon choker with a matching red flower on it that would neatly cover up Mel's henna tattoo.

"It's me!" Mel cried.

"Tell me something I don't know, sugar," Jonah said in a schmaltzy Southern drawl. "Now put that on and go win *Flirt* a Pulitzer. We're seriously overdue for one!"

"Thanks, sweetie!" Mel cried, giving Jonah one of the double-cheeked air kisses he adored. "I'll make sure you get some of the credit from the Pulitzer judges."

"Well, duh!" Jonah said, shooing her out of The Closet.

Laughing, she scurried down the hall, settled herself at her desk, and immediately called her contact number at Florent. She scheduled an interview with the vice president for the next day at Florent's manufacturing plant in Queens.

She felt both exhilarated and shaky all at once.

Let's just hope our little scheme works, she thought, gnawing nervously on a cuticle, a habit she was sure Ms. Bishop would heartily disapprove of.

Suddenly, Mel's computer chortled. Someone was IM'ing her.

When Mel saw the name flashing in her IM window, though, she almost screamed!

    Delia_D: Melanie, are you there?

Are there web cams here? Mel wondered, glancing around the office shiftily. Spotting no electronic eyes scrutinizing her, she bit her lip and typed her reply.

    Mel_H: Of course, Delia.
    What can I do for you?

    Delia_D: Ms. Bishop would like
    to know if you've made all your
    arrangements for your Florent story.

Breathing a sigh of relief, Mel happily typed:

    Mel_H: Yes, I did! I just got off

the phone with Florent. I'll be
interviewing Addison Filpin, the
VP in the perfume division,
tomorrow morning.

Delia_D: Good. Come to Ms. Bishop's
office immediately, please.

Mel's mouth dropped open. She gaped at her computer screen.

"Oh no!" she whispered to herself. "This cannot be good. Somehow, some way, Josephine Bishop is onto me!"

ⓖ   ⓖ   ⓖ   ⓖ

Mel couldn't believe she was approaching Bishop's office for the third time this week.

In all my years of school, she wailed inwardly, *I've never been to the principal's office this many times.*

But wouldn't you know, Bishop was about to surprise her again.

"Melanie!" she said when Mel peeked through her office door. She was sitting on one of the cowhide chairs, examining an array of papers on the coffee table. "Come in, come in. Sit down."

Then Bishop did something even *more* stunning.

She smiled.

"Ready to work?" she asked brightly.

"Of course!" Mel said. "Um, on what?"

Bishop's smile dimmed, but only a bit.

"As you were told on your first day at *Flirt*, one of your duties as the Features intern is to assist me with all aspects of the paper's written word," she explained. "Periodically this summer you'll work at my side, line editing the copy that's come in, going over assignments for this month's book, and looking at proposals my editors have made for next month's book."

"Sounds great!" Mel said. "I have just one question. What's this 'book' you're talking about? I mean, aren't we working on the magazine?"

Bishop's smile faded even more, but a shred of it remained as she said, "We in the industry, Melanie, refer to the magazine as 'the book.' "

"Oh!" Mel said, turning pink. "Well, um, break out the book, then. I'm ready to start when you are!"

ⓖ   ⓖ   ⓖ   ⓖ

The first hour of work was intimidating, to say the least. Bishop began by giving Mel a sheaf of beauty blurbs to line edit at her desk.

But Mel, a writer through and through, felt terrible messing with another writer's words. So all she did was correct the most obvious mistakes. Never mind that a good half of the blurbs felt clunky or hackneyed or just plain boring to her.

When Mel tromped back to Bishop's office to hand them in, the editor gave them a quick glance and made an impatient sound.

"Melanie," she declared, "you displayed a lot of edge in your internship application. That's why I gave you the job. But I'm seeing none of that talent here. Now tell me what you *really* think."

Mel tried not to sigh audibly as she walked back out of Bishop's office and prepared to retackle her first blurb. She read it as she walked to her desk.

If the week at work has been running you ragged, the blurb read, *try this assortment of Ambiancé facial masks. The cucumber-herb will give your skin a tingle, while the avocado-oatmeal is très soothing. You—and your pores— will be back in working order before you know it, especially given the fact that the masks dry a mere five minutes after application.*

Meg gaped at the yawner for a moment, trying to conjure up what would make it better.

When she put her red pencil to paper, she found herself starting over from scratch.

Let's face it, ladies, she wrote. *If we reached for soothing facial masks every time we were stressed out, we'd spend our lives walking around with green gunk on our mugs. The truth is, we're too busy devouring food on the run to spend precious time smearing it on our faces. That's why* Flirt *recommends Ambiancé facial masks. In addition to the fact that Ambiancé is known to use cruelty-free testing*

"You've broken about five fashion-magazine rules here."

on their cosmetics, this fruity-smelling stuff dries just five minutes after you slap it on. Which means you can have your avocado-oatmeal mask—and eat it, too.

Mel didn't give herself time to reconsider before thrusting her new blurb in front of Bishop.

"Is this what you had in mind?" she asked.

Bishop read the blurb quickly. And when she looked up from it, a smile was playing around her lips.

"Well, you've broken about five fashion-magazine rules here," she observed, "but you've also written some really snappy copy."

"Really?" Mel cried. It was all she could do not to start jumping up and down. Luckily, it was too hard to jump in her high-heeled sandals anyway. "So, do you think you're going to publish it in *Flirt*?"

Bishop frowned.

"Melanie," she admonished, "I know you're ambitious, but you should focus more on learning this summer than amassing clippings. You have a great deal of talent, but it's raw. You need to find some balance between your voice, your passion, and the rules of the magazine business."

"Sounds like there are a lot of rules," Mel said.

"Hence, all that learning," Bishop said. "You've

got plenty of potential, Melanie. If you're smart with it, you could go far. And that"—Bishop's close-lipped smile returned—"is why I've been so hard on you this week."

After that, Bishop had Mel organize the editors' progress reports on that month's assignments and give rankings to the proposals for next month's assignments. Finally, Mel was ready to turn all her finished work into her editor. When she walked into Bishop's office—which was getting less scary every time she did it—Bishop was sitting on her cowhide couch, drinking a cup of tea with a pile of sugar packets next to it.

I can see why Bishop needs the sugared-up caffeine, Mel thought. *This job is even more grueling than I thought!*

It was also exhilarating.

Just imagine how cool it would be if I could run a magazine the way Bishop does, Mel thought dreamily. *But instead of dishing about next season's hemlines and heel heights, I'd write about things that make a* real *difference.*

Of course, Mel thought as she sat down next to Bishop, *if my Florent story goes the way I hope, I could end up making that difference right here!*

chapter eight

By the time Mel got home that night—after spending her afternoon prepping for her Florent sabotage, er, interview—she was completely wiped.

She wasn't the only one. When she got back to the loft, all of her roommates except Genevieve were sprawled on the couches looking limp and bedraggled.

"Don't even ask me to go bowling," Mel said as she stumbled over to join them. Olivia swung her bare feet over to the coffee table to make room for Mel to flop onto the couch next to her. "Or to go out for dinner. Or to go jogging or anything else. You know I won't be able to say no. But I'm too exhausted to say yes!"

"No worries, girlfriend," Alexa murmured. She was sitting cross-legged in an easy chair, her head resting in her hand. Charlotte was leaning against Alexa's chair, staring into space. "I assisted a photographer on a fashion shoot today," Alexa continued. "I had to hold a giant reflector over my head for three hours. *Three hours*. And every ten minutes I had to shift the angle so the sunlight would hit the model's face *just. So. Ai!* It was maddening."

"I heard Genevieve was so wiped, she ducked out to go shopping," Olivia said in a shocked voice.

Kiyoko snorted.

"Is it just me," Alexa groaned, "or does it feel like Friday? I mean, the week has been so long, I can't believe it's not Friday yet.

And not even *this* Friday. *Next* Friday. I can't believe how much there is to do between now and then. Like three big photo shoots. And that RunCatchKiss fashion show. And my department meeting, not to mention the *inter-department* meeting . . ."

"Okay, you guys," Mel announced, without bothering to lift her head off the arm of the couch. "If Alexa is tired, then that settles it. We're gonna have a Girls' Night In."

Taking a deep breath, Mel hauled herself back off the couch, scooped her purse off the floor and headed for the elevator.

"You guys order some take-out," she instructed her buds, "and I'll get some movies. I'll be back in ten minutes."

"Hey, wait!" Kiyoko cried. "Can you grab something for me while you're out, too?"

"Sure," Mel said.

Kiyoko hauled herself out of her seat and loped over to Mel to whisper something in her ear. Mel grinned widely.

"Excellent idea," she said. "You got it."

ⓖ　　ⓖ　　ⓖ　　ⓖ

An hour later, the girls had perked up considerably. The coffee table was littered with white cartons of mostly-devoured Chinese food and they were twenty minutes into one of the movies Mel had picked up while she was out. It was a vintage Johnny Depp/Mary Stuart Masterson flick called *Benny and Joon*.

"Wow," Olivia marveled as Johnny/Benny showed Mary/Joon how to make grilled cheese sandwiches with a clothes iron. "So there *was* a time when Johnny Depp was cute-weird instead of creepy-weird. And I'm impressed that he's not doing a terrible English accent!"

"Hey," Kiyoko said, looking around the room, "if everyone's done eating, we can move on to phase two of Girls' Night In."

"Hmmm," Alexa said, glancing away from the TV. "Would that have anything to do with that mysterious brown paper bag Mel brought home?"

"Aren't *you* the investigative reporter," Mel said, shooting Alexa a secret wink. Alexa giggled conspiratorially. Kiyoko popped to her feet and headed for the kitchen, calling over her shoulder, "Pause the movie, will you? I'll be out in a sec."

Ten minutes later, she emerged from the kitchen with a bowl and a mini-spatula.

"This is food, but we're not gonna eat it!" Kiyoko laughed. She tipped the bowl forward so her buds could see its contents. "We're smearing it on our faces! Ladies, I give you a homemade mask of egg whites, honey, yogurt, and cucumber."

> **This is food, but we're not gonna eat it!**

"Gee," Mel said, "facial masks seem to be my theme song today."

"You want me to put *that* on my face?" Genevieve protested with a curled lip. "I mean, if it was made by Aveda or Kiehl's or something, okay. But a facial mask by Kiyoko? I don't think so."

Mel watched Kiyoko's expression harden. Not wanting the feel-good vibe of their girls' night in to go south, Mel cut in.

"I bet you," she said to Genevieve, "that after half an hour with that gunk on your face, your pores will be tighter, your skin will be glowy, and you'll be able to kiss your blackheads good-bye."

Mel had a feeling that Genevieve wouldn't be able to resist the challenge. And she was right.

"Okay," Genevieve sighed. "Lay it on me."

While her roommates laughed, Kiyoko smeared a layer of the chunky white gunk over Genevieve's face. Then she moved on to Charlotte, Mel, Olivia, and Alexa. After she was done smearing up all of them, there was just enough gunk in the bottom of the bowl for herself. Olivia helped her slather it on.

"Okay!" Mel announced, fluttering her hands in front of her face to begin drying her mask. "Back to *Benny and Joon*."

"*Benny and Joon?*" said a male voice from behind them. "I love that movie!"

Mel froze. The voice, of course, belonged to Nick!

Blushing mightily behind her chunky white facial mask, she turned toward him.

"Whoa!" Nick yelped.

"Hi, Nick," Mel sighed. She felt *so* stupid. "Um, we're doing a little beauty ritual."

Alexa and Kiyoko grinned at him through their gunk and waved.

"My grandmother always used to tell me," Olivia explained to Nick, "you have to get ugly before you get beautiful."

"I think this stuff looks pretty good, actually," Charlotte said with a laugh, tapping on her mask to see if it had dried at all.

"Y'know?" Mel squeaked. "I think my pores are tight enough. Excuse me!"

ⓖ　　ⓖ　　ⓖ　　ⓖ

"Oh, sooooo romantic," Olivia sighed as the credits rolled an hour later. By then, she and the other girls had washed off their masks and their faces were shiny and fresh-looking. "Love really does conquer all, doesn't it? I mean, Johnny was all kooky and Mary was completely mental, yet they found their common ground over an ironing board stacked with grilled cheese sandwiches!"

"Oh yeah," Kiyoko teased. "Grilled cheese. *Really* romantic. The next time some guy tries to woo me with a bouquet of orchids or some Vosges chocolates, I'm gonna say, 'What? No Velveeta?' "

Olivia laughed hard, proving that the chill between her and Kiyoko had definitely thawed, at least for the moment. Meanwhile, Mel sprang to her feet again.

"Thanks for reminding me, Keeks," she declared. "We need some chocolate! It's the perfect ending to a Girls' Night In. I wonder if there's any in the kitchen."

"Actually," Nick said, unslouching himself from his easy chair, "I happen to know about a secret chocolate stash in the kitchen. My mom keeps it inaccessible so she won't chow on it every day. The woman is an addict."

"Lemme at it!" Mel squealed, dashing to the kitchen. "I promise to stop by a market and replenish Emma's stash tomorrow."

While Nick dragged out a step stool and propped it in front of an extra-tall cabinet, Mel leaned against the counter and sighed.

"I loved the way Joon was an artist in that movie," she said. "Every time she was upset or her mind wasn't working quite right, she could retreat into her paintings. Is it like that for you?" she asked Nick. "Does painting shut the world out for you?"

"Kinda the opposite, actually," Nick said, hopping down from the stool. "For me, painting is about letting the world in. When I paint, it's like I pour out all the stuff I experienced that day—all the sounds and smells and emotions I gathered off the streets of New York."

Nick paused and looked at his hands shyly.

"Which sounds really pretentious, doesn't it?" he said. "I don't know, it's hard to explain."

"Maybe I'd get it if I looked at some of your work," Mel suggested. "I'd love to see it."

"Yeah?" Nick said, his eyebrows raised. "Sure, why not. Come on back to the studio."

Mel was so excited, she wanted to jump up and down. But instead, she grabbed a bar of Cadbury Dairy Milk.

"For sustenance during the viewing," she joked. She and Nick walked to the hallway that led to his suite. Just before they disappeared into the corridor, though, Genevieve's voice chased them down.

"Leaving so soon, Mel?"

Mel froze and peeked over her shoulder at her roommates.

"Oh, Nick was just gonna show me his paintings," she explained, hoping her friends would get the subtext.

Kiyoko and Alexa glanced at each other with raised eyebrows and Olivia grinned widely. Clearly, they *did* get Mel's drift.

But on Genevieve, apparently, the subtext was totally lost. She must have forgotten all about their conversation at Tomoe. She jumped to her feet.

"Ooh, that sounds cool," she said. "Nick, I've been curious about your work, too. Why don't we all go?"

"Really?" Charlotte said, glancing hesitantly at Mel. When Genevieve nodded emphatically, Charlotte shrugged and hauled herself to her feet.

"All right then," Nick shrugged. "I guess we'll have a mass viewing."

Olivia shot Mel a sad glance and mouthed, *Sorry*.

As the seven of them entered Nick's studio, though, Mel's disappointment waned. The large drywalled space was amazing, all littered with massive canvases, paint-smeared palettes, and tubes, pots, and tin cans of wild pigments. Most of all, Mel thought Nick's paintings were incredible! They were almost all huge, with layers upon layers of wildly colored stripes. Hidden between the different pigments were tiny images and sometimes words. These were painted in black, then covered over with a wash of color so they looked ghostly.

Mel loved one of the paintings in particular, a rectangular collection of yellow and orange slashes, interspersed with almost-hidden words in newspaper headline font. The phrases included *population boom*, *one million cars enter Manhattan a day*, and other eco-conscious rants.

Oh my God! Mel thought gleefully. *Nick's a total lib. He'd completely get along with all my boycotting/protesting buds in Berkeley.*

As Mel stared in fascination at the painting, she felt Nick sidle up next to her.

"I get what you mean now," Mel whispered to him. "I feel like this painting is bigger than its canvas. It's like the world out *there* is all in *here*."

Nick's voice was low and rumbly as he thanked her.

"Not everybody sees that," he said, "but that's how I felt when I was painting it."

"Hey, what's that?"

Mel turned toward Alexa's voice. She expected her friend to be pointing at another of Nick's paintings, but instead, she was gazing at a ladder that ran up the wall to a hatch in the ceiling.

"That's the roof," Nick said with a shrug.

"The roof!" Alexa cried. "As in a view of downtown Manhattan? As in a starry summer night? You guys! We've gotta go up there!"

Mel looked at Nick in surprise. He grinned and shrugged.

"It *is* really cool up there," he said.

"Let's go, then!" Mel declared. "I think it still counts as a Girls' Night In if we stay *on* the building."

"And if there's a boy included?" Nick asked with a laugh.

"The right kind of boy only adds to the fun," Mel said. Then she scrambled after Genevieve up the ladder to the roof.

66 Not everybody sees that. 99

◎   ◎   ◎   ◎

As each girl climbed through the hatch onto the

tarry, gravel-strewn roof, she exclaimed at the glittering city view, the night sky that looked so much bigger from six stories up, the sweet-smelling summer breezes.

Only Kiyoko had something different to say. Peering over at the building next door, she called out, "Well, hello, boys!"

Well, hello, boys!

Mel gasped and followed Kiyoko's gaze, just in time to see a large handful of dudes wave back at them from *their* sixth-story roof.

"Hi!" several of the guys yelled.

They all looked to be about Nick's age. Several of them wore T-shirts or baseball caps that said NYU.

"Where did you come from?" asked one of the boys.

"From far, far away," Kiyoko called back.

"Well, you're too far away at the moment," the guy answered. "Why don't you folks hop over? Have a beer."

He motioned at the cozy scene he and his friends had set up—a large semicircle of lounge chairs with a cooler and a folding table of snacks in its center.

"Um, not to be a buzz-kill, you guys," Nick called back, "but these girls are sixteen and they're living here with my mom. If they start drinking and my mom finds out I just sat there and watched, I'm dead."

"So don't watch," Kiyoko cooed. "C'mon, boys! Lend a hand."

She hopped fearlessly up to the shallow ledge at the edge of the roof. Charlotte yelped in fear, but Kiyoko winked at her.

"There's only, like, twelve inches between these two buildings, Charlotte," she said. "It's nothing."

As soon as the flirty guy gave Kiyoko his hand, she leaped lightly across the divide and landed on his roof. He handed her an amber bottle and led her to the rest of the group.

"Oh, why not?" Olivia tossed off. She scampered to the roof's edge and jumped across herself.

One by one, all the girls made the leap until only Charlotte, Mel, and Nick were left.

"Charlotte," Nick assured her. "You don't have to do this if you don't want to."

Could Nick be any more caring? Mel thought as she nodded in agreement.

But Charlotte was biting her lip and gazing at Genevieve, who'd already struck up a smiley conversation with a guy in an expensive-looking shirt and a preppy haircut. Charlotte set her jaw in determination.

"I wanna go," she said. "I'm not gonna be a chicken this whole summer."

"Okay," Mel shrugged. "We'll help you, right, Nick?"

"Absolutely," Nick agreed. They each took one of Charlotte's arms and led her to the ledge. Charlotte started quaking before they even stepped up to the lip.

"Let's do this fast," Nick said, gazing over Charlotte's head at Mel. "On the count of three, we all jump. Okay?"

"One, two, *three*!" Mel yelled. She did it so fast that the three of them crossed over the narrow chasm before Charlotte had a chance to hesitate.

"I did it?" Charlotte squeaked, looking around in disbelief. "I did it!"

After doing a little victory dance, she gave Mel a quick hug and trotted over to share the news with Genevieve. Mel noticed that Charlotte also dipped into the cooler and pulled out a beer.

"I prefer," Mel said to Nick with a wry smile, "to celebrate with Cadbury. Wanna square?"

> **" I prefer to celebrate with Cadbury. "**

"Sure," Nick said. "We did some good work there with Charlotte. We deserve a little sugar."

Nick grinned as Mel broke off some chocolate for each of them. Then they sauntered over to join the party.

❍　　❍　　❍　　❍

Within an hour, the NYU boys and the *Flirt* interns were the best of friends. Every one of the boys had tried his hand at flirting with Kiyoko, only to be rebuffed with ever-more-creative barbs.

And when Kiyoko was done teasing them, they moved on to Charlotte, who responded with hysterical laughter.

Maybe, Mel realized, *being on her third beer is helping a bit.*

Nick gave Charlotte a worried look. Then he jumped off his chair and stretched.

"Well . . ." he said, "I better hit it. I've gotta work the breakfast shift tomorrow."

He gave Mel a pointed look. Mel grinned back, loving the silent communication between them, even if it wasn't the romantic spark she'd imagined at the beginning of their evening.

Chemistry is chemistry, she consoled herself, *and Nick and I clearly have it. There'll be other opportunities to catch some alone time. Maybe even when we say good night . . .*

The idea was so exciting that Mel jumped out of her own chair.

"Me too," she said with an exaggerated yawn. "C'mon you guys. You ready? *Flirt* awaits!"

Olivia, Kiyoko, Alexa, and Genevieve nodded and got up to join Mel.

The *Flirt* girls thanked the NYU boys for the picnic and began to hop, one by one, back to their own roof. It was no surprise that, once again, Charlotte was the last one left.

But this time, she wasn't determined.

Or brave.

No, she was simply drunk. She stood several feet away from the edge of the roof, wringing her hands and sobbing.

"I can't," she cried. "I'm too scaaaaared."

Genevieve wasn't amused. She called across to Charlotte, "If I were you, I'd calm down. You don't want Emma—and therefore my Aunt Jo—to know you were drinking, do you?"

Charlotte's eyes widened in horror. With great effort, she stopped crying.

Then she squared her shoulders, gritted her teeth, and made a run for the edge of the roof. She was going to jump.

But a few steps before she reached the edge of the neighboring building, Mel saw her face change.

In a very bad way. She'd squeezed her eyes shut.

"Charlotte!" Mel cried. "You're going blind! Open your eyes!"

But apparently Charlotte was too scared, or inebriated, to comply. With her eyes still tightly closed, she made a wild leap.

And suddenly, Mel was glad Charlotte couldn't see. If she could, she would have known that she was falling right for the narrow chasm between the buildings.

"*Ay ay ay!*" Alexa screamed.

"Catch her!" Olivia cried.

Nick didn't say a word. He was too busy saving Charlotte's life. As her arms flailed, her toe caught on the lip of the roof next door. Nick scrambled toward her, slipping a bit on the gravelly roof.

Charlotte began to fall.

And so did Nick! He landed on his knees as she skidded into the edge of his roof, then thrust out his arms toward Charlotte.

"Ooof!" Charlotte grunted as she landed—squarely in Nick's outstretched arms. Her midriff was stretched over the space between the buildings, but with her legs still caught and her arms firmly in Nick's grasp, she was—somehow—safe.

Finally, Charlotte opened her eyes.

And when she saw what had happened, and what had *almost* happened, she *really* lost it, breaking out into a fresh round of sobs. Nick dragged her over to their building. They both sat on the ground, Charlotte wailing and Nick patting her shoulder and rubbing his knees, which were surely badly scuffed beneath his denim pant legs.

"Oh my God, Charlotte!" Genevieve screamed, racing to Charlotte's side. "How could you be so stupid?"

"You told me I'd get in trouble!" Charlotte wailed. "I was just trying to do the right thing!"

As Genevieve shook her head and began stalking back to the roof hatch alone, Mel stared after her.

Sure, that's not the smartest thing Charlotte's ever

done, Mel thought. *But shouldn't her best friend be a little more sympathetic? What's up with Gen?*

Olivia was being much nicer to poor, weeping Charlotte.

"Don't you worry, darling," she said, leaping to Charlotte's side and wrapping an arm around her shoulders. "We'll help you down that ladder. We won't let anything happen to you. And now maybe you'll steer clear of that stinky American beer?"

"You know it," Charlotte nodded tearily.

Mel sighed with relief as Olivia and Alexa led Charlotte to the hatch and began to help her down the ladder. Then Mel peeked back at the forbidding space between the two buildings and shivered.

She couldn't help but think about her "mission" to the Florent Company the next morning. Officially, she'd be there to interview the vice president of the perfume division and a few other VIPs. But at the same time, she and Alexa would be searching for evidence of the company's cruelty to animals.

Part of her couldn't wait to test her journalistic chops.

But another part of her wondered if she was about to plunge into something as dark and dangerous as that six-story chasm.

chapter nine

"**A**nd *that*, girls, is how we do a perfume launch! Now, as for sales figures . . ."

It was Friday morning and Mel and Alexa were in a swanky office at the Florent Company's plant in Queens, enduring the most boring lecture Mel had ever heard. They were only about halfway through their interview with the perfume division's vice president, Addison Filpin, and already Mel knew there was almost nothing in the interview she could use in her feature. Still, she diligently kept her digital voice recorder pointed at Filpin's nonstop mouth and tried to look interested.

It'll help with our mission, Mel thought slyly. She glanced at Alexa, who was stalking around Filpin's polished chrome desk, snapping the occasional picture of him. Filpin, a paunchy man with rosy cheeks and graying temples, was clearly loving Alexa's attention. He practically preened for the camera, all the while maintaining eye contact with Mel and talking to her earnestly.

"Say, Mr. Filpin," Alexa said suddenly. "You know what would really help our story? Some shots of the lab where you develop your perfumes. You know, where you do testing . . . research and development. That sort of thing."

Harrumphing as he hauled himself out of his chair, Filpin led the girls out of his posh office on the industrial building's second floor. He took them to a staircase, which led to a bare-bones lobby on the ground floor, and used a laminated card to buzz them through a door.

Now they were in a hallway that was anything but posh. It was a long stretch of linoleum with fluorescent lights buzzing overhead. Their trio passed door after glossy white door. About half of these doors featured brushed chrome signs that said things like RESEARCH AND DEVELOPMENT: LIPSTICK AND FOUNDATION or PRODUCT PHOTOGRAPHY STUDIO or HERB AND PIGMENT STORAGE.

But the other doors weren't labeled at all.

Intriguing, Mel thought. Before she could decide what to do about these mystery doors, Filpin was using his key card to unlock another door. This one was labeled NOSE ROOM.

"Nose room!" Mel said with a grin. She almost expected to see a line of noses mounted on the wall. Instead, there was just a quartet of men and women, all wearing white lab coats and bustling around with test tubes, glass vials, and other scientific-looking stuff.

"Girls," Filpin announced, "meet our 'noses,' some of our most valuable assets here at the Florent Company."

66 She almost expected to see a line of noses mounted on the wall. 99

"Hello!" said one of the noses, a tiny woman with frizzy blond ringlets and, appropriately enough, a hawk-like nose. "I'm Emily Gardner."

A man strode up as well and introduced himself as Stuart Alden—in a voice so nasal, Mel had to wonder if he had a horrendous cold.

Must be hard being a nose when you can't smell anything, she told herself, coming dangerously close to laughing again.

Instead, she busied herself with pulling out her voice recorder. The noses sat down at a lab table.

> **"Is it okay if I ask you a few questions?"**

"Thank you so much for having us here," Mel said to them as Alexa began snapping pictures. "Is it okay if I ask you a few questions?"

Ꮐ   Ꮐ   Ꮐ   Ꮐ

While the two noses filled Mel in on their scent development methods, it was hard for her to peek around the lab in search of animal-abuse evidence.

The problem? The noses were actually interesting.

"Most people probably imagine us crushing up rose petals and cedar chips and the like to get our scents," Gardner told Mel. "But did you know that petals have nothing to do with a flower's scent? It's all about oils emitted in the heart of the flower . . .”

The road from raw odors to a polished Florent perfume was a long and fascinating one. Mel soon found herself immersed in the conversation, despite herself.

Besides, a quick glance at Alexa, who was photographing everything and everyone in the room, assured Mel that Alexa was doing an excellent job of snooping on her own. So Mel allowed herself to focus fully on the interview.

Besides, she *did* have one question relevant to her investigation.

“So you say you divided scents into musks, florals, citrus, and woods,” Mel said to the noses, repeating back to them what they’d told her. “Then you spent months mixing the scents into different combinations before arriving at the final combination that would become this new perfume, Thoughtful. Then what?”

“Oh, well,” Gardner said with a shrug, “then I suppose they hire designers to come up with the bottle and advertising specialists to design a launch campaign. But we don’t have anything to do with that. We’re just the science geeks of the operation.”

“Well, isn’t there anything else you need to do?” she prodded. “Say, to test for the safety of the perfume? I mean, I thought every product on the market had to be tested for allergic reactions, skin irritations, and stuff like that?”

Mel saw her two noses exchange a furtive glance.

Then she noticed that the other two science geeks—the ones who'd been busy with their glass vials in the back of the lab—had stopped bustling and cocked their heads to listen.

"How *do* you test for, say, skin allergies or eye irritation?" Mel asked, widening her eyes innocently.

"Of course, there's safety testing," Alden said brusquely. "The Florent Company tests each and every one of its products to ensure the consumer's safety."

Hmm, is he quoting the perfume packaging directly? Mel wondered cynically.

"Testing happens in another lab," Gardner volunteered. "I'm afraid it's as boring as this one. A bunch of test tubes and slides and such."

"In any case, it's not our area," Alden said abruptly. "You probably can't understand this, being only a teenager, but in the corporate world, the division of labor is very succinct. We have our role. Testers have their roles. Marketers and executives have theirs, et cetera. You can't possibly expect us to tell you the inner workings of every department in this vast company."

Mel pursed her lips.

"That's a tough concept to grasp," she said sarcastically, "but I'll try to wrap my teenage brain around it."

"You do that," Alden said, getting to his feet and stuffing his hands into his lab-coat pockets. "Now, if you'll excuse us, we have to get back to work."

" You can't possibly expect us to tell you the inner workings of every department in this vast company. "

"I understand," Mel said, getting to her feet as well. She turned to a chair in the corner, where Addison Filpin had been waiting—or perhaps supervising?—during her interview.

"Mr. Filpin," Mel proposed, "perhaps you can take us to talk to the testers?"

Filpin jumped to his feet.

"Eh, what was that, Melanie?"

"Well, as Mr. Alden was just saying—"

"That's Dr. Alden," the nose sniffed.

"Sorry, *Dr.* Alden," Mel corrected herself, "I've been lucky enough to speak with you, Mr. Filpin, from Florent's executive division. And now, Drs. Gardner and Alden from the development area. But in order for my report to be complete, I'll really need to speak with a perfume-safety tester—and perhaps someone in your marketing department as well?"

Filpin shook his head. "Well, I'd love to, Melanie," he said jovially, "but when you called, you requested ninety minutes here at Florent, and that time is up. Tell you what, here's a card for our head of marketing. You can call her and do a phone interview."

"Great!" Mel said. "And a tester?"

"Okay!" Filpin said, clapping his hands together and beckoning to Alexa. "It was wonderful to have you here. We're thrilled about the story and, of course, very impressed with you accomplished young ladies."

"But," Mel began to protest, "Mr. Filpin, you haven't answered my ques—"

"All ready!" Alexa announced, suddenly materializing at Mel's side and squeezing her upper arm painfully.

"Ow!" Mel exclaimed in surprise.

Alexa looked deep into Mel's eyes—and continued to stare at her—as she repeated herself.

"I think I got some great shots, Mel," she said carefully. "We're *all done here*."

In short order, Filpin led the girls back down the corridor and into the lobby. He pointed them toward the front door.

"Just leave your visitor passes with the security officer on the way out," he instructed them.

"No problem," Alexa said. "But before we go, can you point me to the ladies room?"

"Uh, certainly," Filpin said, going a bit pink. "Here, it's right near the stairwell. I'll point it out to you as I head back up."

While Alexa traipsed away with Filpin, Mel slumped against the marble wall of the lobby, feeling sulky. Filpin had done a fabulous job of deflecting her questions about perfume testing, and Alexa had totally given him a helping hand.

Not thirty seconds after Alexa had left, she came scurrying back to Mel.

"That was a fast bathroom trip," Mel pouted. "Ready to go?"

Alexa pointed at the door to the hallway.

"Did you see all the unmarked doors?" Alexa said. "It could be a gold mine."

"A locked one," Mel complained, pointing at the electronic lock next to the hallway door. "Filpin used a key card to get through there."

"Mel," Alexa said with an eye roll, "you underestimate my abilities as a sneak."

With a devilish grin, she reached into the waistband of her pants and pulled out a white, laminated card.

"Oh. My. God," Mel cried. "Have I told you today that you are a goddess?"

"Save the compliments for later," Alexa scoffed. "We've got investigating to do."

ⓖ   ⓖ   ⓖ   ⓖ

As Alexa used her stolen key card to get back into the long, white hallway, Mel's heart thumped. She could hear the blood rushing in her ears, too. Part of her was so terrified, she wanted to just turn and run.

Another part could only think about those red-eyed bunnies.

And Filpin's shifty eyes.

And the challenge Bishop had issued to her in her office the day before: "Tell me what you *really* think."

Mel gritted her teeth, grabbed Alexa's hand, and pointed at the first unmarked door in the hallway. Looking both ways, Alexa bit her lip and slid the key card into a small panel next to the door. A light in the panel flashed from red to green.

Mel and Alexa gazed at each other, their eyes wide. Mel reached out and turned the doorknob. Then, holding their breaths, the girls jumped inside.

"Well, *that's* an anticlimax if I ever saw one," Mel sighed, gazing around the room. There was nothing there but a bunch of file cabinets. "Although I guess we could come back and rifle through these if we can't find anything better. Maybe there's some records in here or something."

"Sure," Alexa said sarcastically. "I've got a week to camp out here and search every piece of paper they've got, don't you?"

"Good point," Mel said. Let's move on . . ."

ᕗ   ᕗ   ᕗ   ᕗ

"This is it," Mel said with a frown. "The science wing. This is where all chemical and otherwise gross operations clearly happen. This has gotta be it."

"If there *is* an it," Alexa added.

Feeling her heart go back into thump mode, Mel grabbed the key card from Alexa, marched over to the unmarked door, and slid it into the key-card panel. The red light turned green and Mel thrust the door open.

"Ah!" she cried.

Unlike all the other doors they'd opened on this hallway, this one led to a steep staircase—one that descended into a gloomy-looking basement.

And together, the girls began to tiptoe down the stairs.

"What do we do if there's someone down here?" Mel whispered to Alexa over her shoulder.

"Why are you asking me, drama queen?" Alexa said. "You'll just invent a tale, that's what!"

Mel nodded, but she did so with a shiver of fear. With each step down the metal staircase, Mel could see more scary-looking stuff. She spotted a metal shelf filled with plastic tubs, bottles, and canisters, many of which were marked with red skulls and crossbones. There were several pieces of unidentifiable, industrial-looking machinery. Mel also spied a metal table that looked like the examining table at the vet where the Hendersons took their fifteen-year-old cat.

When the girls descended the final step, they saw one more door to the right of the staircase.

And one more key-card panel.

Mel and Alexa didn't have to speak. The grim knowledge hung between them—a second locked door, down in this creepy basement, meant Florent had something to hide.

Mel pressed her ear to the door before she unlocked it. Luckily, she didn't hear any voices.

Any human voices, that was.

She *did* hear several muffled cheeps, squawks, and screeches.

Biting her lip, Mel swiped the key card and pushed the door gently open.

Then she gasped.

Alexa brought her camera to her face so swiftly, it thunked against her forehead. Alexa didn't even seem to notice. She was too busy *click-click-clicking* away.

Mel, on the other hand, stood frozen for a full minute, staring.

Staring at the cages.

There were too many of them to count. They lined three walls of the lab and were stacked on top of each other until they almost reached the ceiling. Inside were guinea pigs with big patches of missing fur, mice scratching compulsively at their ears, and rabbits whose eyes were red and watery.

After another horrified moment, Mel became aware of Alexa's busy clicking. She remembered that she had a job to do as well. Hanging from each cage was a small clipboard. Mel grabbed her notebook out of her purse and pounced on the first clipboard she saw. It was all she could do to scribble down the content of the file—

rather than fling open the cage door and reach inside to comfort the shivering guinea pig.

But Alexa's *click-click-click* kept Mel on track. She noted that the guinea pig had been smeared with high concentrations of a Florent moisturizer-in-the-making.

A rabbit next door to the guinea pig had been subjected to an eye-makeup remover.

Mel scribbled and moved to the next cage, scribbled and moved to the next cage. After recording six or so awful experiments—but finding none that were related to Thoughtful perfume—Mel began skimming over the clipboards quickly. If she could just find evidence linking this horrendous testing to Thoughtful, Mel knew she could convince Bishop to run a negative story about Florent.

Or no story at all, Mel realized with a cringe.

Not getting articles into *Flirt* hadn't exactly been her goal when she'd applied for this internship.

But some things, Mel reminded herself, *like the welfare of these poor animals, are more important than my career.*

Mel moved onto a new bank of cages—ones that gave her hope of finding what she was looking for. On one clipboard was the name of a Florent perfume she recognized: Amorous. On another was a men's cologne called Green.

"I'm getting close to being done," Alexa whispered to Mel, her camera still clicking away. "I just need a long

"Mel forgot herself and screamed."

shot of this room and then I think I've got more than enough damning evidence."

As Mel continued flipping through the clipboards as fast as she could, Alexa began backing away. She kept her camera to her eye, carefully adjusting the composition of this most important photo—the photo that would depict Florent's entire animal lab in all its grisly gory.

Alexa shuffled backwards. *Click-click.*

And a little more. *Click-click.*

Just a little more—

Crash!

Alexa had backed into a rickety metal shelf stacked with food bins. Two of the large containers tumbled to the ground next to Alexa's feet. The noise so startled her, she jumped.

And *that* only jostled the shelves again. Six more food bins crashed loudly to the cement floor. About half of them flew open, spilling bits of animal kibble everywhere.

Mel forgot herself and screamed.

The animals squeaked and squawked in alarm.

Alexa moaned as she rubbed the spot where a bin had crashed into her shoulder.

And finally came the worst sound of all—that of two security officers crashing into the basement lab, shouting, "Put your hands over your heads!"

The next thing Mel knew, the girls were back in Addison Filpin's office. But this time, they weren't guests.

They were prisoners.

Okay, I guess that's an exaggeration, Mel admitted as she and Alexa squirmed in chairs in front of Filpin's desk. *It's not like we've been cuffed or anything. Although, to tell the truth, I'd face handcuffs over Josephine Bishop's wrath any day.*

Too bad Filpin hadn't given Mel that choice. In fact, he was on the phone with Bishop at that very moment.

"Yes, that's right," he was saying, his nostrils flaring and his ruddy face bright red. "They *stole* a key card and snuck into highly classified areas of the Florent Company. Ms. Bishop, this is an outrage and you may be hearing from my lawyers—what was that? Oh, yes, ma'am. My pleasure."

Filpin grinned as he turned to Mel.

"She wants to talk to you," he said.

No, Mel wailed inside.

She took the phone from Filpin with a shaking hand.

"Ms. Bishop, I can explai—"

"Not a word, Miss Henderson!"

Mel's mouth closed with an audible clap.

"You clearly have no understanding of what you've

done," Ms. Bishop said. "But let me assure you, you are in deep, *deep* trouble. Now I want you in my office in half an hour."

"Yes, Ms. Bishop," Mel stuttered. "But we're in Queens. It took as an hour and two different trains to get out here—"

"Just be here!" Bishop barked. "Or you can kiss your internship good-bye."

Mel was shaking harder when she hung up the phone.

"*¿Que?*" Alexa asked her. Her tan face had gone sallow and pale and her lips were thin with tension.

"We need to be there in thirty minutes," Mel whispered.

"But how?" Alexa wailed. "Impossible!"

"We do have a car service you could use," Filpin said, a hard little smile splicing his ruddy face. "Trust me, we'd be happy to help you take your leave of the Florent Company. Of course, the charge for this service is sixty-five dollars, before gratuity. And I don't think Florent *or* Flirt is going to foot the bill."

Mel gazed miserably at Alexa. That was a lot of money. But what choice did they have?

⊚   ⊚   ⊚   ⊚

Mel and Alexa arrived in Bishop's office in about twenty-nine minutes, thirty seconds. They'd run so hard through the Hudson-Bennett lobby and *Flirt* offices, they were gasping when they arrived.

As they quivered in Bishop's doorway, their editor glared at them. Her nostrils flared, just like Filpin's, but her skin was as creamy and pale as always.

She opened her mouth to begin what Mel was sure would be a long lecture. But before she could utter one word, a man shoved into the office from behind the interns. He was about five feet six inches tall, though he had a wild shock of white hair that added at least three more inches to his frame.

Ms. Bishop glanced at Mel and Alexa and said with a curled lip, "Girls, this is Henri Auberge, the president of the Florent Company."

Mel felt her face fall.

Bishop went to her bar and poured Auberge a brandy. Then she led him to one of her cowhide chairs.

Naturally, Mel thought, curling her lip at the cowhide.

Bishop sat next to the old man and spoke to him in low tones. As he replied, still clearly angry, she nodded vigorously and patted him on the shoulder.

Only after he'd drained his snifter of amber liquid and shot a few more ugly glares at Mel and Alexa did Auberge finally nod and get to his feet.

"Josephine," he said in a thick French accent. "I hope you'll keep a tighter rein on these *enfants* from now on."

"*Absolument*. I promise, Henri," Bishop responded, looping her arm through Auberge's to lead him to her office door. "I'm so sorry about this."

The moment the door closed behind Auberge, Mel leaped to her feet, wringing her hands.

"Ms. Bishop, I want you to know this is all my fault!" she cried. "Alexa was just helping me with my plan. Please don't blame her for this."

"Frankly, you both deserve to be sent home for this little stunt," Ms. Bishop spat. "But since it *was* Melanie's assignment . . ."

Mel gripped the edges of her chair. *Sent home?*

"I'm so incredibly sorry, Ms. Bishop," she croaked. "I . . . I thought you'd actually be proud of me for taking initiative. Being a real reporter. Writing from my passion. I *never* thought my plan would be so . . . destructive. Is there anything I can do to change your mind?"

Ms. Bishop paced silently before the girls for a long, agonizing moment. While Bishop frowned in thought, Mel gnawed on her cuticle and thought, *If I lose this internship, I'll seriously die!*

Then a taunting voice piped up from the back of her mind: *Well, a few days ago you thought you'd seriously die if you had to write a puff piece about the Florent Company. So which is it, Henderson? Your internship? Or your ideals? What's more important to you?*

I don't know, Mel answered silently. *Why can't I have both? Why?*

For the first time, Mel realized that those writers from *The New Yorker* and *Harper's* that she so admired might not actually be living the life of artistic purity she'd envisioned. Maybe it had taken them more than just talent and passion to get where they were.

Maybe Mel needed more than that, too. She needed to play by the rules.

Clearly, using charm and her wits to wiggle out of little scrapes was no longer working. And now she was in danger of knocking herself out of the magazine game— for good.

What have I done? Mel thought in anguish. *How could I have been so dumb?*

Mel was so immersed in her internal angst that she jumped when Bishop began to speak.

"Let me impress upon you how serious this matter is," she began. "Not only have you embarrassed this magazine, and me personally, you've put us in grave danger. The Florent Company, with whom *Flirt* has enjoyed a very good relationship for a very many years, has threatened to pull all its advertising from the magazine. You can't even begin to understand the financial blow this would be to *Flirt*. Now, I think I talked Henri out of it, but I can't be positive."

Suddenly, Mel flashed on something Jonah had said as he'd given the girls their tour of The Closet earlier that week.

"Stella, Calvin, Miuccia, Donatella . . . we're the best

of friends," he'd said, pointing at the clothes. *"We feature their frocks in our fashion layouts—and they advertise with us. It's one big back-scratch over here, and we all benefit!"*

Mel felt herself wilt.

Florent wasn't just using Flirt *to promote its perfume.* Flirt *got something out of it, too—money that it clearly needs to keep operating.*

"Melanie," Bishop announced in her clipped voice, "I don't know what kind of magazine you want to write for, but at the moment, you work for *Flirt*. This is no place for gonzo journalism. In attempting this *infiltration*, you have disrespected our magazine. And the Florent Company. You've hurt your fellow interns, particularly Alexa. You've embarrassed me. You've . . ."

Mel listened miserably as Bishop went on and on and on.

"I also find it hard to believe, Melanie," she said, "that you would make this foolish move after the work we did together the other day. Perhaps I misjudged you."

Mel looked at her with tears in her eyes.

"No, I think you judged me correctly," Mel said sadly. "I was incredibly naive. I guess I just had a dream that writing for a magazine would be different. I thought I could write purely about things I believe in. But I realize it's not so black and white."

And I still don't like it, Mel thought. *But do I have a choice in the matter?*

She didn't have *any* choices, she knew, if she lost

the internship.

Maybe if I can stay at Flirt *and try again,* Mel thought, *I can do good work without breaking the rules. Maybe that's what I really need to learn this summer.*

With all her energy honed on saving herself, Mel said, "I'll do anything if you'll give me a second chance, Ms. Bishop. I'll even write the Florent story you wanted. I did get some really good quotes from the noses I interviewed."

> **"I'll do anything if you'll give me a second chance, Ms. Bishop."**

"It's too late for that," Bishop declared. "There will be no Florent article."

Oh my God, Mel moaned to herself. *Here it comes. My pink slip! I can't believe I didn't even survive one week at* Flirt *magazine.*

"But," Bishop added, "you will not be going home to California, either. I'm sorely tempted to punish you that way, but . . . well, Melanie, you're nothing if not honest. I believe that you didn't think you were doing something wrong. Your intentions were good, even if they were terribly misguided."

Melanie clenched her fists in hope.

"To compensate for your mistakes, you are to spend the weekend in my office," Bishop declared to Mel, "doing some filing tasks that have been piling up for months. You're very correct, Melanie, to point out that *Flirt* magazine is not just a summer adventure. It is also a business. One that you have endangered."

Yes! Mel thought. She'd been psyched about spending the weekend exploring the far reaches of New York City, but at the moment, filing away her sins in Ms. Bishop's office sounded heavenly.

"And," Bishop added, "you *will* be filing a feature to me. Since you are so intent on doing your own work, you will come up with the topic. But it had better be in keeping with the tenets of *Flirt* and it had better be brilliant. Otherwise, I might have to reconsider your internship assignment. Perhaps you'd prefer something less challenging, like sorting through the letters to the editor or compiling the fashion credits in the back of the book."

Mel hung her head and nodded.

"I really appreciate this, Ms. Bishop," Mel rasped. "I won't disappoint you. Again."

"I should hope not," Bishop said. "And Alexa? Your beauty-product shots were excellent. Expect to do more of them next week. *Many* more of them."

Alexa hung her head as well.

"Yes, ma'am," she whispered.

Completely shamed, Mel and Alexa slunk out of the office. The moment they'd cleared Delia's desk, Mel whispered, "I'm *so* sorry, Alexa!"

"It's not your fault," Alexa waved her off. "And besides, we're still here. You still have the chance to wow Bishop with a story—one that's *not* about bunny torture.

And, as far as I know, Bishop has no intention of calling my parents and telling them about our little adventure. Which means no harm done."

"I guess you're right," Mel said glumly.

But as she tromped across the cube farm to her desk, it was hard to have Alexa's faith. Mel was more confused than ever. Had she just sold her soul to hang on to her internship?

Or had she done the right thing?

Mel had wanted to be a journalist her entire life. But now she realized she'd never really understood what that meant. She'd thought it was all about writing beautiful prose and changing the world. But now, she could see that it was also about making a product that attracted advertisers and could be sold to consumers.

Not unlike a perfume company, Mel realized.

Mel was no longer certain that magazine journalism was the right place for her. On the other hand, she wasn't ready to chuck it all yet.

She couldn't let go of her dream without a fight.

Which means, she warned herself, *I have to keep myself in the running by writing an incredible article for Bishop. If I fail, Bishop is fully capable of letting everyone in the magazine industry know that I'm unhireable. After all, the woman is massively connected.*

So basically, Mel thought as she slumped into her chair, *my entire future rests on this article. No pressure or anything!*

chapter ten

W hile Mel's roommates slept in the next morning, Mel crawled out of bed at seven, intent on getting to her filing early. When she tiptoed to the kitchen to grab some breakfast, she found Emma at the table sipping a cup of tea. She was wearing yoga pants and her hair was woven into two braids.

"Ready for work?" Emma asked sympathetically.

"So you heard," Mel groaned. She shook her head sorrowfully as she fished three toaster waffles out of the freezer. "I can't believe what a mess I made of things yesterday."

"Sounds familiar," Emma said with a little smile.

"What, did one of last year's interns completely sabotage herself, too?" Mel asked, popping the waffles into the toaster.

"No, that would have been me," Emma said. She slurped at her tea. "Back when I was a fashion photographer at *Flirt*, Ms. Bishop requested some very simple fall fashion shots. White backgrounds. Studio lighting. Models staring directly into my lens."

"What do you do instead?" Mel asked, immediately seeing where this was going.

"Oh, I fancied myself a young Annie Leibovitz," Emma said dryly. "I took the models to the Museum of Modern Art. I decided

I'd tell a story about the season's angular hemlines by posing them against some geometric sculptures. I did exactly the opposite of what Ms. Bishop asked for. While I can't say the photos were *bad,* I can say they were wrong. Wrong for *Flirt*."

Mel felt a guilty twinge.

"So what happened next?" Mel said.

"Oh, another photographer did the studio shots," Emma said. "I was exiled to the darkroom for a couple of weeks before I went back to shooting. It was all fine. I could have stayed on at *Flirt* forever, I guess. But about a year after that incident, I decided to leave the magazine to become an art photographer."

"Couldn't take the compromises, huh?" Mel said. She pinched her waffles out of the toaster, doused them with syrup, and shuffled over to the table to join Emma.

"No, that wasn't it," Emma said, slurping at her tea. "I just realized that fashion magazines weren't the right place for me. Even though that's what I'd dreamed of ever since I was, like, twelve."

"Huh!" Mel said.

That sure sounds familiar.

"The cool thing about this internship, Mel," Emma said, draining the last of her tea from her cup and getting

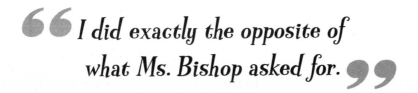
I did exactly the opposite of what Ms. Bishop asked for.

to her feet, "is not only will you learn a ton about the biz, you'll also learn about yourself. About what you really want. And what you're meant to do." Emma continued as she thunked her cup into the dishwasher, "The challenge is recognizing the writing on the wall when you see it."

> ❝ **The challenge is recognizing the writing on the wall when you see it.** ❞

Emma's so right, Mel thought. *That* is *the biggest challenge. Knowing what I now know, do I still want to be a writer? My gut tells me I do. But is that just because this has been my dream since I was ten?*

Emma broke into Mel's thoughts as she padded toward her suite.

"Well, I'm off to do my yoga," she said. "Have a good day, Mel."

"I'll try," Mel called after her.

She felt jealous of Emma's serenity. Her compromise-free life as an art photographer.

But then she flashed back on something Emma had just said.

"About a year after the incident . . . I realized fashion magazines weren't the right place for me."

It took Emma a whole year to come to that conclusion, Mel reassured herself. *I shouldn't expect to have all the answers after a few days. For now, I need to focus on doing my filing and coming up with a kick-butt story for Bishop. I can get all existential next week.*

Then Mel smiled grimly as she polished off her waffles and headed out of the loft.

◎　　◎　　◎　　◎

Luckily, the filing Mel had to do was so detail-oriented that she didn't have time to think about anything else. Her first major task was to photocopy every article in the previous year's issues of *Flirt*, then divide the articles by category, then laminate them and arrange them in binders. She also had to number these pages and create an index of the articles in a computer file.

It took her all day.

Which meant her other major tasks—filing Bishop's internal correspondence into computer folders and dividing a giant stack of glossy photographs into dated folders—would have to wait for Sunday.

Which meant on Sunday, Mel arrived in the office at seven thirty in the morning, wearing her most tattered pair of capris, an orange tank layered over a completely clashing purple one, and some blue flip-flops that didn't match, either.

She worked so hard that by noon her eyes felt like they were crossing and her stomach growled violently. Hoping against hope that the caf was open on Sundays so she could grab a quick sandwich, Mel grabbed her wallet and shuffled toward the elevator.

When it hummed open, Mel gasped.

Because lurking inside were Alexa, Olivia, Kiyoko, Genevieve, and Charlotte.

"We've come to steal you away for brunch!" Alexa giggled. "Kiyoko made reservations at Balthazar."

"B-but, I don't have time!" Mel said. "I have so much work left to do here."

"That's why I'm coming back here with you after brunch," Alexa declared. "To help you out. After all, you didn't get into this spot alone.

"Alexa," Mel said. "This is my responsibility. You totally don't have to—"

"Enough!" Alexa said, dragging Mel into the elevator. "Balthazar awaits."

Mel giggled and allowed her friends to kidnap her. As they rode the elevator down to the lobby, she noticed that every one of them was swanked out in Sunday-cute outfits.

"Um, I don't know what this Balthazar is," Mel said, "but I'm thinking my ratty old capris and tanks are wildly inappropriate garb for it?"

"Wildly," Olivia said sweetly. "And we don't care a

" We'll just hide you behind the *fruits de mer* platter and nobody will notice a thing. "

whit. We'll just hide you behind the *fruits de mer* platter and nobody will notice a thing."

"Har-har," Mel said sarcastically. But her smile was real. As she and her buds hailed a cab headed downtown, Mel felt her shoulders untense for the first time in days. Even if she couldn't erase the stress of the coming afternoon—not to mention the coming week—her friends were going to help her put it on the back burner for at least a couple of hours.

"You guys," Mel declared as their cab barreled down Fifth Avenue, "are the best!"

ⓖ   ⓖ   ⓖ   ⓖ

And Balthazar was indescribable. From the moment Mel set foot in the bustling French bistro, she felt transformed from a scruffy teenage intern into a glamorous New Yorker. She fell in love with Balthazar's tiled floor and sepia mirrors, its marble bar and cramped tables filled with beautiful people nibbling on crab legs, mussels, and eggs in puff pastry.

As the hostess led the girls to their table, Charlotte squeaked, "Oh my God, you guys. Johnny Depp is sitting at the corner table!"

As usual, Kiyoko rolled her eyes.

"That *so* isn't John—oh my God!"

Mel followed Kiyoko's gaze to the corner table. A man with long, scraggly hair and yellow sunglasses lounged in a booth, unapologetically smoking Gauloises. All around the restaurant, people were stealing looks at the star and trying to pretend they weren't.

"Yup!" Mel crowed. "That's Benny, all right. Burn, Kiyoko!"

She expected Kiyoko to respond with her usual snarky retort. But instead, Kiyoko had gone pale and breathless.

"No. Way," Mel laughed. "We've finally seen a crack in Kiko's cool!"

"Ha!" Alexa exclaimed. "We've finally discovered someone who could conquer Kiko's heart! And his name is John—"

"His name," Kiyoko interrupted with a scowl, "is Matteo!"

"Who?" Olivia said. "I haven't heard of that star."

"He's not a star," Kiyoko said. "He's my boyfriend and the love of my life. We met at my international school in Tokyo. I miss him like crazy. Why do you think I'm so indifferent to every one of the guys who wants me in this city?"

Mel and the other girls gaped at Kiyoko.

Then they collapsed onto their table and filled hip and trendy Balthazar with their howls of laughter.

"I cannot *wait* to write about this in my journal!" Mel squealed. "First a crush on Johnny Depp, now a secret boyfriend. Keeks, you're priceless!"

"And you're not writing a word of it!" Kiyoko

threatened. But there was a laugh behind her voice, too. "Let's just eat. I'm starving!"

ⓖ   ⓖ   ⓖ   ⓖ

Once the girls' laughter had died down, Mel quickly decided to order the brioche French toast, a couple of eggs, and a large cappuccino, even if it would amount to a twenty-five-dollar breakfast. She wanted to live this two-hour break to the fullest. She couldn't have been happier.

Until she spotted a familiar face in the crowd. A familiar face that was making its way toward the girls' table.

Alexa, noticing that Mel was sinking into her seat, looked up from her menu.

"Lynn!" she exclaimed. She waved Lynn Stein, photography editor, over to their table. In the glow of the Sunday-morning sun that filled Balthazar, Lynn looked incredibly relaxed. On her arm was a sweet-looking, portly man.

"Well, hi, girls!" Lynn said. "This is my husband, Steven. Stevie, meet our new *Flirt* interns. Aren't they cute? I see you all are having a quintessential New York brunch. Even you, Mel! I heard you were working in Ms. Bishop's office all weekend."

"We made her come!" Alexa defended Mel. "She's been slaving away since the wee hours of the morning."

"Alexa," Mel grunted through clenched teeth, giving Alexa—who was sitting next to her at the crowded table—a little kick.

"No worries," Lynn said, waving away Mel's worried face. "This is the adult world, sweetie. We don't care when or how you get your work done. As long as it gets done. Kinda nice, isn't it?"

"Kinda a lot of responsibility, too," Charlotte pointed out glumly.

"It's all part of the territory," Lynn said, nudging her husband in the belly with her elbow. "Right, honey?"

"Get used to it, girls," Steven confirmed, slinging his arm around Lynn's shoulders. "It's all downhill from here."

"Stevie!" Lynn reprimanded him with a laugh. Then she turned to the interns. "Okay, he *might* be right. There's a lot of stress in our little magazine world. But there are rewards, too! Like the *Flirt* fashion show on Tuesday night, for instance. It's all about fall ready-to-wear. Very important."

"Can't *wait*," Olivia burbled. "I've got a new Tuleh dressed picked out just for the occasion."

"It'll be a lot of fun." Lynn nodded. "Well, we're off to a matinee. See you girls at the office!"

As Lynn and Steven plunged back into the crowd, holding hands, Mel turned to Olivia in a panic.

"That fashion show is on Tuesday night?" she cried. "The one that's sponsored by RunCatchKiss? The *big* one?"

"Melllll," Kiyoko admonished her. "You still haven't finished reading through that orientation folder, have you? It's on our schedule of events. Hello, we've been talking about it all week. Jonah's all aflutter about it."

"Indeed!" Olivia said. "Where do you think I got the Tuleh dress? From The Closet. And then Jonah showed me how to do this wild thing with highlighter. You guys, I actually had cheekbones!"

Mel cut her off with a wail.

"I don't know why it didn't register that it was on Tuesday," she complained. "I was gonna go to Nick's art opening on Tuesday."

"So go!" Genevieve proposed. "I mean, what's more important to you, Miss Serious Journalist? A fashion show? Or spending your summer with an arty boyfriend who lives in the suite next door?"

"As if it's a sure thing!" Olivia sputtered, shooting Genevieve a glare. She turned to Mel. "Mel, we all sense the chemistry between you and Nick. But it's also true that he didn't invite you to the show. Maybe he wants to focus on his art there. Remember, my parents own a gallery. I know how stressful these openings can be for artists. You'll have plenty of other chances to make a play for Nick."

> ❝ You'll have plenty of other chances to make a play for Nick. ❞

"Yeah, but not one this dashing!" Mel said. "Even if he doesn't have time to hang with me, I think he'll still be touched that I showed up. It'll be the perfect way to show him how I feel."

"True," Kiyoko admitted. "But the fact is, you can't go. You *have* to go to the fashion show."

"Especially when you're on such thin ice at *Flirt* already," Alexa said, her usually sparkly eyes clouded with worry.

"Okay," Mel agreed ruefully, propping her chin on her hand. "What time is this lip-glossy thing, anyway?"

"Um, seven thirty, I think," Kiyoko said. "Then there's a cocktail party afterward, and after *that* is the after-party, and—"

"Wait a minute," Mel said, perking up. "Seven thirty? Nick's show at the Ryan Gallery is from six to nine. I Googled it and found out the dets. So if I go to the gallery right when the party starts—"

"Unfashionably early?" Genevieve noted.

"Hello?" Mel replied cheerfully. "I think we've established that I'm not so fashionable, haven't we? The point is, I can do both! I can spend, like, an hour at the opening, then hightail it to the fashion show."

"I don't know," Olivia said with a frown. "Sounds like you're cutting it very close."

"Liv," Mel cooed, draping her arm around Olivia's

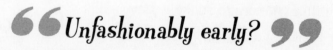

66 *Unfashionably early?* **99**

shoulders, "I've been in New York almost a week. Are you implying I haven't figured out how to get myself around this city? Why, I've even been to Brooklyn and back."

"You have?" Genevieve said. "When?"

"Remember when I was late getting back from Bowlmor?" Mel said through a giggle. "It's called missing your subway stop!"

"So you weren't out partying after all," Gen accused.

"No," Mel admitted. "I'm not fashionable, *or* a party girl."

"You are the coolest, though," Alexa said, giving Mel a quick hug.

"I'm also famished," Mel said, looking at her menu. "I wonder where our server is. I'm thinking of adding the crepes du jour to my order, too!"

⊚   ⊚   ⊚   ⊚

The brunch ended all too quickly. While Kiyoko, Olivia, Genevieve, and Charlotte sat back in their chairs, reapplying their lip gloss and chatting about what to do with the rest of their day, Mel reluctantly got to her feet to leave. She felt incredibly grateful when Alexa made good on her promise and jumped up to join her.

"Bye, you guys," Mel said, waggling her fingers at her buds. "I *hate* to go."

They'd almost made it to the frosty-glassed door

when Mel felt her toe connect with something squishy.

Then that squishy something went skidding across the tile floor.

Mel gasped. She'd just punted someone's purse! In all the bistro's chaos, she hadn't noticed it, tossed casually on the floor next to a booth. As the little lime green Marc Jacobs pouch sailed across the slick floor, the stuff inside fell out in a steady stream.

"Oh no!" Mel cried. Without a moment's hesitation, she fell to her knees and began chasing after the purse, gathering up its contents as she went.

She picked up a couple of lipsticks, a cell phone, a breath spray, a BlackBerry, and a package of Kleenex before she located the purse itself. Hurriedly, she stuffed all the goods back inside and trotted it back toward the booth.

It's my collision with Nick all over again, Mel thought, trying not to laugh. *Not to mention the time I almost got plowed down by a pizza guy and a socialite in a limo, all in the same day. Let's see how I get out of* this *New York moment.*

Mel arrived at the booth. Alexa was standing there waiting for her, visibly squirming. She looked like she wanted to duck under the nearest table, in fact.

When Mel made to return the purse to the woman sitting in the booth, she realized why Alexa was so uncomfortable.

The woman—who was surrounded by a bunch of

bored, Eurotrash types—was spitting mad.

She was also . . . familiar.

"Hey," Mel said as she handed the purse over. "Aren't you the comedian from that reality show, *The E List*? You're Katie Pippin!"

"Duh!" the woman said, snatching her purse back. She sneered at Mel. Well, as much as she *could* sneer. Her lips were so collagen-pumped, they were practically immobile. "Learn to watch where you're going, missy! The youth are so careless these days."

Around her, Katie's hangers-on tittered compliantly.

That's when Mel started to get mad.

It wasn't the low-level celebrity's snottiness that pushed her over the edge. It was this entire superhard, screwup-riddled week.

Mel's frustration bubbled up in her chest. She was sick of messing up. From the Florent Company debacle to her weekend of busy work to this stupid purse-kicking incident, she just couldn't seem to get a break.

Which never happens to me! Mel protested in her mind.

Mel was totally angry with herself—for being impulsive and reckless when she had such an incredible opportunity; for thinking she knew how to be a journalist when, clearly, she had a ton yet to learn; for trusting that when she screwed up, she would always land on her feet.

If this Katie Pippin incident proved anything, it was that Mel couldn't always count on good luck to get her through life.

She'd have to rely on her wits.

Starting, Mel ordered herself, *right now* . . .

"Gee, that's funny, Katie," Mel snapped at the still-snickering celeb. "If you hate 'the youth' so much, why do you keep getting all that plastic surgery to make yourself look younger? Doesn't really make sense, does it?"

While Katie Pippin's superlifted eyes widened and her cheek implants went slack with shock, Mel grabbed Alexa's hand and marched the two of them out of Balthazar. Then she stalked up to the curb, threw out her arm, and howled, "Taxi!"

A cab screeched to an immediate halt.

"Hudson-Bennett building, please!" Mel barked as she and Alexa climbed inside.

Inside the cab, Alexa gazed at Mel with wide, admiring eyes.

"Wow," she said. "I guess you *can* make your way around New York after all!"

chapter eleven

"**U**m, excuse me, guys? Can I get through? Hello?"

Mel was standing in the doorway of one of the loft's bathrooms, where Genevieve, Charlotte, and Kiyoko were primping madly. They were so intent on their beautifying, they barely noted Mel's presence.

In the other bathroom, Olivia was in the shower and Alexa's beauty supplies were arrayed all over the vanity.

Mel was shut out.

As usual.

On any other evening, this would not have been a big deal. Mel would have brushed her teeth in the kitchen sink, slapped on some scented oil in her bedroom, zipped a comb through her hair, and gone on her merry way.

But this wasn't any other evening. This was Tuesday night! The night of Nick's gallery opening.

And, oh yeah, Mel reminded herself, *the RunCatchKiss fashion show, too.*

It all added up to one thing—Mel had to look fabulous.

And since her event was a full ninety minutes before her roommates' event, she also felt it was fair to pull rank.

"All right!" she announced. "I have to be at a gallery in

Chelsea in exactly forty-five minutes and I'm coming in!"

Mel reached into Olivia's shower and turned the water off. Then she tossed Olivia a towel and began peeling off her own clothes.

"Outta there, Bourne-Cecil!" she said with a laugh in her voice. "I'm in crisis mode."

"Cheeky," Olivia protested, stepping out of the shower with her fluffy towel wrapped around herself. "You're just lucky I've already rinsed the conditioner out of my hair, Henderson, or you'd be in for it. But, are you sure you still want to do this crazy scheme?" she asked, sounding worried.

"What's crazy about it?" Mel said from behind the curtain. "All I need to do is leave the gallery in Chelsea by seven. Then it's a fifteen-minute subway ride to the fashion show on the Upper West Side. It'll be as easy as running, catching, kissing. Mmmm, kissing! Maybe tonight will be the night that Nick and I finally lock lips!"

"Well, if you do," Olivia quavered, "just don't lose track of time! You can't afford any more slipups at *Flirt*."

"Olivia," Mel protested as she began shaving her legs, "was Bishop not completely satisfied with my weekend filing? Did I not edit, like, ten pages of copy yesterday, prompting Bishop to send me an e-mail extolling my attention to detail? Did I not spot a typo that a *host* of editors had missed at today's editorial meeting?

"I'll just have to save being brilliant for tomorrow!"

The typo that turned the word *flick* into . . . well, another word entirely?"

"Yessss," Olivia droned.

"So, don't worry," Mel said jovially.

She was saying this as much for her own benefit as Olivia's. Because, in her list of the past two days' accomplishments, there was one glaring absence.

I haven't yet come up with an idea for a brilliant story for Bishop.

Mel bit her lip as she finished rinsing off and stepped out of the shower. The only thing that could distract her from her gnawing worry over this matter was the clock on the bathroom wall. She had half an hour to get to Nick's opening.

Which means, she told herself as she began brushing out her wet hair, *I'll just have to save being brilliant for tomorrow!*

◎ ◎ ◎ ◎

Mel stepped out of a cab in front of the Ryan Gallery at six fifteen. But she didn't kick herself for being late. That extra fifteen minutes of primping had made Mel look pretty dazzling, if she did say so herself.

She'd blown her hair instead of letting it air dry

> ## 66 *I don't know how I'm going to go back to life without The Closet.* 99

into its usual twisty turny waves. Now it hung down her back—a sleek, blond-streaked curtain.

She'd rubbed iridescent lotion on her limbs so her skin almost glowed in the night air.

Her pink, flowy, strapless dress fit like a fluttery dream.

Finally, Mel had forgone her usually flat flip-flops and tied on some shimmery, high-heeled, Grecian sandals with laces that crisscrossed around her ankles.

All she'd needed to complete the look was a gauzy pink wrap and a tiny clutch purse that perfectly matched her shoes.

I don't know how I'm going to go back to life without The Closet, Mel thought, tightening one of her pearl drop earrings and grinning.

Then she braced herself for a Nick sighting and strode into the gallery.

◎　　◎　　◎　　◎

Fifteen minutes later, Mel *still* hadn't spotted Nick.

She *had* managed, however, to run into a dizzying array of Art Schmoozers. First there'd been a couple in bizarre glasses. The woman wore lime green hexagons and the man tiny, blood red rectangles. They were having an argument in front of a painting of a cubist nude.

"Please, will you settle this argument for us," the woman said, ensnaring Mel before Mel could sidle away. "I think this painting is derivative of Picasso, and Mr. Art History Ph.D. here thinks it's derivative of Schnabel. What do you think?"

"I think . . ." Mel quavered, "that it makes me hungry. And ooh, there's the hors d'oeuvre guy! Can you excuse me?"

Mel hadn't just been lying to make her escape. As always, she *was* hungry. And she *had* seen a waiter passing by with a tray of something yummy-looking.

Unfortunately, the waiter seemed uninterested in Mel. She trotted after him as he skimmed through the crowd. And when he didn't stop, she tapped him on the shoulder.

"Excuse me," she said, "are those treats on your tray vegetarian?"

The waiter turned to her, a sarcastic sneer in his hard blue eyes.

"Why, yes," he declared, "they are."

Then he turned on his heel and walked away, without giving Mel a chance to pluck one of the hors d'oeuvres off the tray.

Mel huffed in frustration before she spotted another waiter a few feet away.

"Yes," she whispered, practically running to catch the guy.

Which was why it was such a surprise when Mel ran right into Nick. She smacked into him so hard, in fact, that one of the deep-fried hors d'oeuvres he was nibbling went flying out of his fingers, coming dangerously close to grazing the painting he was looking at. He managed to hang on to one of his artichoke puffs.

"Mel!" he gasped, holding the artichoke puff awkwardly in front of him.

"Nick!" Mel gasped back. "I'm sorry! I wasn't even paying attention to where I was going."

"Yeah, I've experienced that before," Nick said with a smile. "Although I didn't expect to crash into you here."

"Oh," Mel said, laughing nervously. "Well, I heard about your opening, and you know, I really loved your paintings when I saw them the other day . . ."

Suddenly, Mel felt more than nervous. For the first time since hatching this storm-Nick's-art-opening plan the previous week, she began to wonder if she'd done the right thing.

But it was too late to backtrack now. And besides, Nick looked so luscious in his fitted, snazzily striped shirt and his sleek black pants that she just had to press on.

"The truth is," Mel said nervously, "I didn't come here just for the art. I came—because of you."

"You . . . did?" Nick said. He looked stunned.

"I did," Mel said quietly. She smiled shyly. And suddenly, she was transported straight into her fantasy, in which a grateful, love-requiting Nick had gathered her in his arms, not caring that they were surrounded by abstract art and obnoxious schmoozers, and given her a soft, sweet kiss.

Mel was so immersed in this fantasy, in fact, that she took a purposeful step toward Nick. She lifted her face toward his. She pursed her lips into a pre-kiss pucker. Then she lifted her arms to wrap around his neck and—

"Mel!" Nick said in alarm. He held up his hand, which was still clutching his artichoke puff. "Wait!"

But it was too late. Mel was leaning in for the kiss. There was no stopping her.

Okay, maybe there was one thing stopping her. A hot and greasy sensation pressing right into her abdomen. Gasping in surprise, Mel took a step backward and gazed down at her dress. Squashed right into the beautiful, pink, gauzy fabric covering her stomach was Nick's greasy, flattened artichoke puff. The puff stuck there for a moment before peeling off her dress and falling to the floor. It landed with a splat, leaving an egg-sized grease spot on her dress.

Mel looked up at Nick, her mind roiling with confusion. He looked just as bewildered. He looked from the empty cocktail napkin in his hand to the hors d'oeuvre on the floor.

"Oh my God," he sputtered. "I'm sorry."

"No, *I'm* sorry," Mel jumped in, hating how shaky her voice sounded. "Clearly, that was the last thing you wanted me to do."

"No!" Nick exclaimed. "I mean, *yes*. Well, it's kind of complicated, you see—"

"There you are!"

A girl's voice—throaty and brimming with flirtation—jutted between Mel and Nick. The owner of the voice, a lithe, dark-skinned, black-haired girl who looked to be about Nick's age, quickly followed. She slunk right up next to Nick, snaked her slender arm around his waist, and pressed against his side possessively.

"I couldn't *find* you," the girl complained, brushing her lips against Nick's neck. "I kept getting intercepted by hors d'oeuvre guys. They were, like, foisting their greasy food on me. Yuck."

"Um, Mel?" Nick said. Now he was the one with the shake in his voice. "I'd like you to meet my girlfriend, Anastasia. Anastasia? Mel. Mel's one of the *Flirt* interns. You know, my mom's their house mother?"

Anastasia stopped nuzzling Nick's neck to give Mel a heavy-lidded stare. Mel felt her face go bright red.

Okay, Mel thought. *While my dress is pink and babyish, hers is black and poured on like paint. She's as tall as I am, but she also looks like a Brazilian supermodel, one who's definitely older than sixteen and surely has no need for a housemother.*

So, to sum up: Anastasia? Queen of the World. Mel? Not so much!

Mel emerged from her thoughts more depressed

than ever.

Meanwhile, Anastasia cocked her head and gave Mel a curious look.

She totally knows I want her b.f., Mel realized, her face going hot.

"Well . . ." Anastasia said, nicely but firmly, "it was nice meeting you, Mel."

Mel didn't know what to say. No matter what she said, she knew she'd come off looking pathetic.

So she didn't say anything. Instead, she shot Nick one last confused, longing look, turned on her kitten heel, and ran. She couldn't believe she'd been so deluded as to think Nick could be interested in her.

Well, I think that's screwup number twenty-five or so for the week, Mel grumbled, kicking herself inside. *A new record!*

It felt better to be mad at herself than to let her true emotions surface. But there was no denying that, underneath her anger, her heart was broken. All she wanted to do was go home and burst into tears.

It was only when she emerged from the gallery that she remembered she *couldn't* go home. She had a fashion show to go to. And, Mel realized when she glanced at her watch, she was late.

"No!" Mel cried out loud. *Make that screwup number twenty-six.*

By the time Mel got to the Upper West Side and found her way to the hotel where the fashion show was being held, it was 8:05.

But it's a fashion show, Mel told herself as she rushed through the lobby and breathlessly asked a concierge to point her toward the main ballroom. *A fashion show stocked with diva models, petulant designers, and snappish hair and makeup people. It couldn't possibly have started on time, could it?*

Apparently, Mel realized when she reached the doorway of the ballroom, it could. And it had. As Mel sidled through the crowd standing around the door, the show seemed to be in full swing. Music was pumping. Lights were flashing. Models were stalking, dead-eyed, down a long runway set high above the audience.

Mel barely glanced at the models and their artful clothes. Instead, she scanned the audience to see if she could spot anyone from *Flirt*.

It wasn't hard. In one of the best seats in the front row sat Josephine Bishop. She was staring down each model with steely eyes, her mouth set in a grim line. Every once in a while, she jotted notes in a little notebook. And once, Mel saw her twist in her seat and crane to look at something behind her.

Mel followed her gaze—and gasped.

About four rows behind Bishop were Mel's fellow interns, all sitting together. Between Kiyoko and Alexa was an empty chair.

On that chair was a sign emblazoned with a name in bold letters: MELANIE HENDERSON—FLIRT.

"Noooo!" Melanie groaned under her breath. "I am so dead."

Almost hyperventilating, Mel pushed through the crowd of people near the door and hurried up an aisle to her row. Then she tried to edge herself toward her seat. But the chairs were crowded and the spectators' pointy-toed high heels were all in the way. When Mel tried to step timidly over a few pairs of knobby knees, she was greeted with angry hisses.

"There's no room to get through," whispered a woman with a severe, blood-red pout.

Flummoxed and defeated, Mel edged back out of the aisle and slunk to the back of the room.

When the fashion show finally ended, Mel knew she should seek out Bishop and explain herself to her. Then she should have sought out her buds and told them what had happened at the Ryan Space.

But it was all too humiliating. And Mel was way too tired and depressed to handle any of it.

I'll deal with this tomorrow, she thought as the first two tears squeezed out of her eyes. *Things will look better tomorrow. I'll go to Bishop's office first thing in the morning and I'll make it better. Somehow.*

And then, because she didn't have the strength to do anything else, she found an exit door at the back of the ballroom, hailed a cab outside the hotel, and went straight home, falling into her bed and crashing immediately into a fitful sleep.

＠　　＠　　＠　　＠

The next morning, Mel woke up before all her roomies.

Even after a good night's sleep, things didn't look any better than they had last night at the fashion show. Mel dreaded facing her roommates. And she was terrified of dealing with Bishop.

Mel still just wanted to escape. So she slipped into a pair of shorts, a sports bra, and some sneakers. Then she grabbed her Rollerblades and tiptoed out of the loft.

After a quick subway ride, Mel finally felt like she could breathe. That was because she was standing at the entrance to Central Park.

And I thought Greenwich Village was gorgeous, Mel marveled as she gazed at the scene. She delighted in the park's sea of green, its undulating pathways, its cute benches, and the food vendors walking around with umbrella'd carts.

Taking a deep breath of the leafy air, Mel quickly changed into her skates. Then she tied her shoes together, slung them over her shoulder, and took off.

She whizzed through the park, going this way and that, not even caring which direction she took. Every way she turned, after all, led only to more beauty and more cool stuff to see, from a giant Alice in Wonderland statue to a fenced-off spot called Strawberry Fields.

Mel felt her head clearing. She even began to look on the bright side.

I can send Bishop an e-mail today, she assured herself, *and apologize for being late to the fashion show.*

And as for Nick? Well, at least I didn't actually *kiss him. And it's not like I was doing anything skanky. I mean, I didn't know he had a girlfriend! I was totally innocent.*

In fact, she went on, her theory gaining strength, *maybe Nick is the one who should be embarrassed. I mean, he never mentioned his girlfriend. Why was that? And there was chemistry between us. I know it and I think he does, too. So maybe* he's *the one who was acting shifty. Hmmm!*

Before Mel could weave any more conspiracy theories, she skated into a huge circular courtyard with a giant angel-topped fountain in its center and a pond nearby. The courtyard was lined with benches and hosted several food vendors.

One of them was selling protein-laced smoothies.

That reminded Mel that she hadn't eaten in ages. She never had snagged any hors d'oeuvres at the gallery. And after the back-to-back Nick and fashion show debacles, Mel had forgotten all about dinner. She'd gone straight to bed.

Now she skated straight to the smoothie vendor and ordered the largest, most calorie-packed smoothie on his menu. Then she skimmed over to a sun-dappled bench, flopped onto it, and gratefully began to drink her breakfast.

As she enjoyed the sun on her face and her sweet-tart smoothie, two young women sat down on the bench next to Mel's. They both wore long, pale blue jackets that looked vaguely like lab coats. Their hair was perfectly coiffed and their make-up was thickly and impeccably applied. Each girl sipped at a large coffee as they dished away.

"Okay," said the girl with the short, spiky hair. "So first I took some Viva Glam, right? And then I diluted it with some frosty pink? Then I added a touch of gold shimmer and mixed it all into the beeswax. But for the *pièce de résistance*, I put it all in the microwave for eight seconds. It got the stuff melty but not cooked. It's the perfect lip gloss."

"DIY it, baby," said the spiky-haired girl. She sighed and took a sip of coffee. "So depressing, isn't it? Slaving away at the Trista McElroy counter at friggin' Macy's when the stuff we whip up is so much better. Well, at least we can spread the word to the masses through our blog. C'mon, we're gonna be late to work."

It was only after the girls had disappeared from her view that Mel suddenly gasped.

"Oh my God!" she cried out loud. "That's it! That's my story!"

Mel was going to write a story about DIY makeup and perfume. She'd write about people who took their scents and makeup into their own hands instead of buying conformist (and rodent-persecuting) cosmetics from a corporate giant. She'd write about a generation of women who rejected the idea of looking and smelling like everybody else.

The beauty of the story was that the DIYers didn't concoct their cosmetics from scratch. They used stuff like Kiehl's lotion and M.A.C. lipsticks to make their one-of-a-kind wares. That would make *Flirt*'s advertisers happy.

And Mel was sure it'd be pretty easy to find women and girls who didn't test their homemade beauty products on animals. Which would make *her* happy.

As Mel began skating back toward the subway, she thought of one more element that could make her article perfect: Minnie Porter-Haywood, the socialite who'd rescued Mel from Brooklyn on her first night in New York. Her cosmetics company, Minnie Me, represented a young woman taking her DIY thing to the next level. The fact that Minnie was a celebrity didn't hurt, either.

The story was absolutely perfect for *Flirt*.

Mel couldn't wait to get to the office to tell Ms. Bishop all about it. She was so psyched that, after racing back to the loft, she rushed through her morning routine. She showered quickly, threw her hair into a scraggly ponytail, and jumped into an outfit that had been crumpled on her bedroom floor since she'd worn it a few days ago.

When she got to the office, there was a stickie waiting for her on her computer screen.

Please see me. J. Bishop.

Perfect, Mel thought as she hurried through the cube farm. *I can tell Bishop all about my idea now and start my research immediately.*

ⓖ ⓖ ⓖ ⓖ

The only problem with Mel's plan? It was kind of hard to tell Bishop about her stellar story idea while Bishop was busy bawling her out.

"Where were you last night?" she demanded the moment Mel stepped into her office. "Your chair at the fashion show—a chair that had been reserved specifically for you—sat empty all night. It was an embarrassment to this magazine!"

"I'm sorry!" Mel blurted truthfully. "I was a little late and I couldn't make it to my seat without getting in everybody's way, so I just watched the show from the ballroom door."

"You were late!" Bishop stated. She began pacing in front of Mel. "Tell me, Melanie, do you have such disdain for this magazine that you can't be bothered to show up to one of its most important events on time? That you can't seem to run an iron over your clothes before you come to work? If you disrespect *Flirt* so much, why did you apply for this internship?"

"I—I don't disrespect *Flirt* at all!" Mel protested. "Quite the opposite, actually!"

Mel blinked in surprise as she realized that what she'd just said was true. A week ago, she'd thought of *Flirt* as lightweight, as just a stepping stone en route to a more serious career.

And maybe she still did want that career as a world-roving reporter. But she no longer saw *Flirt* as just a rung in her ladder. She knew it was a worthy experience in its own right.

And she wanted to prove that to Bishop by writing the best story ever.

"Let me show you how much I think of *Flirt*," Mel begged her editor. "I've come up with a story idea that I think is perfect for the magazine. Perfect for me, too! I really think you'll like it. It's—"

"Spare me your pitch," Bishop said, holding up her hand. "I don't want to hear another word out of you, Melanie. Just write the thing and have it to me first thing Friday morning. I'll give you no guarantee that it will run in the magazine. But if I like the story, I'll give you a chance to write something for the next issue. That is, *if* you can keep up with the other duties and responsibilities that come with being a *Flirt* intern."

"Thank you," Mel croaked. Hope and panic were mixing it up in her throat.

"Melanie," Bishop snapped as Mel reached for the door. "This is your last chance. I expect you to make the most of it."

chapter twelve

Mel walked back to her desk in a daze and collapsed into her chair. All around her, her friends' heads popped up. They looked like gophers peeking out of their nests.

A moment later, Alexa, Kiyoko, and Olivia were standing around Mel in a tight semicircle. Mel gazed up at them blearily.

"What's going on?" Olivia demanded. "Where were you last night?"

"And what happened with Nick?" Kiyoko asked.

"And what did Bishop say?" Alexa cried. "You were just in her office, weren't you?"

Mel didn't know which question to answer first.

"Well," she began, "here's what happened—"

"Wait!" Kiyoko whispered, holding up her hand. She glanced furtively at a nearby desk, where Genevieve was sitting stock-still, her head angled, her fingers hovering quietly above her keyboard. It was plainly an eavesdropping pose.

"Let's take this chat to the caf," Kiyoko suggested quietly. "We'll have more privacy there than we do here, even if we're surrounded by dozens of Hudson-Bennettons."

The three girls whisked Mel to the cafeteria and got her a plate of comforting baked goods.

"We didn't have to wait on line for this stuff at all!" Alexa joked. "Now if we'd gotten you an oil-free egg-white omelette, it would have been another story."

Mel couldn't even laugh at Alexa's quip. But she was grateful for the pastries. Sighing between nibbles, she told her friends everything. She described the gaffe with Nick's girlfriend and her late appearance at the fashion show, her revelation in the park that morning, and the drumming down she'd received from Bishop.

"And now," she finished, "I have to write this entire feature in forty-eight hours. With a broken heart,"

"And an enemy," Alexa said darkly.

"What?" Mel said, wide-eyed.

"Oh, Mel," Kiyoko scoffed, stealing a bite of Mel's danish. "You're too *nice*. But you can see now that Genevieve's been playing you, can't you? Just as we suspected."

"Who first encouraged you to reject Bishop's Florent assignment?" Alexa noted.

"And who encouraged you to go to the art opening?" Olivia said with an indignant frown. "I bet Genevieve knew Nick had a girlfriend."

"You think?" Mel gasped. "But why would she do that?"

"Jealousy, plain and simple," Kiyoko said. "Genevieve clearly has a crush on Nick, too. It's so obvious. And as for your Features internship and your relationship with 'Aunt Jo'? Hello?"

Mel was horrified. The fact that Genevieve might have deliberately sabotaged her? Well, *that* was too evil for Mel to wrap her brain around.

"So what do I do now?" Mel cried, gazing at her friends with wide eyes.

"About Genevieve?" Olivia said. "Nothing! She's not worth the effort it would take to exact revenge. You are the bigger girl here, Mel. And I don't just mean your height."

"Well, maybe there's something we could do," Alexa said with a sly smile. "We should exclude her from our plan."

"What plan?" Mel asked.

"Our plan," Olivia said, exchanging smiley glances with Kiyoko and Alexa, "to help you with your story. I'm going to stage a photo shoot."

"Really?" Mel squealed. She jumped to her feet and wrapped each of her buds in a muffin-sticky hug. "But what about your stuff? Don't you guys have deadlines to meet, too?"

"After doing product shots all week," Alexa said with a grin, "Bishop told me I could try one photo shoot with models, *if* I can find models who will work for free."

"I'll work for free," Kiyoko said, running her hand over her mane of black hair.

"Me too!" Olivia said with a grin.

"You can't afford me, sweetie," Mel joked. Alexa punched her on the arm and giggled.

Kiyoko and Olivia had also finished enough of their work to help Mel set up some interviews. Mel asked Kiyoko to track down the DIY-cosmetic bloggers she'd spotted at the park that morning.

"It shouldn't be too hard," she said. "They work at the Trista McElroy counter at Macy's. One of them has black hair with purple highlights and the other one has short, spiky hair, bleached blond. They were total buds. I'm sure if you just call up Macy's someone will recognize their description. Or you can Google their blog."

"What, don't you have something challenging for me?" Kiyoko joked.

Mel asked Olivia to talk to some of the funky makeup artists she'd worked with on fashion shoots in the past week.

"I bet you anything they mix makeup to form their own colors," Mel said. "See if anyone will want to go on the record about that. Meanwhile," Mel said with a smile, "I'm going to call upon one Minnie Porter-Haywood and see what she has to say about the DIY movement."

"Ladies," Olivia said, getting to her feet, "I think we've got ourselves a project!"

By the end of the day, Mel was starting to think that she might not have to pack her bags and book a plane ticket back to Berkeley. Because her research was going fabulously.

Minnie, for one, was thrilled to hear from Mel and agreed to meet her for lunch that very afternoon. Over teeny-tiny sandwiches at the Ritz-Carlton, Minnie said, "Honey, please! Nobody who's anybody just uses makeup as it's sold in the stores. It's all about mixing it up. Chanel meets Lancôme meets Bonne Bell Lip Smackers. The rules are *off*. That's why I decided to come up with my own company. Hard Candy cosmetics started the movement, and I'm taking up the torch. Speaking of which . . ."

"*It was exactly what Mel was going for.*"

Minnie reached into the large, expensive tote she'd lugged into the Ritz's tea room and pulled out a black canvas portfolio. When she unzipped it, Mel caught her breath. The portfolio was lined with makeup: pots of face powders; blushes in beautifully subtle colors; shimmery, multicolored eye shadows; and lipsticks arrayed in palettes that just invited mixing and matching.

It was exactly what Mel was going for.

"Take it," Minnie offered, placing the heavy

collection in Mel's lap. "You can use it for your photo shoot."

ⓖ   ⓖ   ⓖ   ⓖ

When Mel arrived back in the office, Olivia reported, "Not only did I get some stellar quotes from Sha-Say—who's a very famous and flamboyant hair and makeup man—but he's also insisted on coming to our photo shoot and making us look DIY-wonderful."

"Yes!" Mel cried. Then she squinted at Olivia, who'd clapped a hand over her mouth. "What's wrong?"

Olivia glanced at Genevieve's desk. When Mel followed her gaze, she saw Genevieve staring back at her, looking wildly curious.

"There's going to be a photo shoot?" Genevieve said, trying to sound casual. "What are you guys up to?"

Olivia shrugged and said to Genevieve, "Oh, it's nothing you'd be interested in. Thanks for checking in, though!"

Then she turned back to Mel to dish—in whispers—about the interview with Sha-Say.

As soon as Mel had collected all of Olivia's notes and added it to her growing stash of research, Kiyoko sent her an IM.

```
Kiyoko_K: Hey, babe. So guess who
I tracked down? The DIY girls
```

themselves. Their names are Missy
Altshul and Veronica Prouty.
Check out their blog, it's HI-
larious. Definitely good for a
quote or two: www.potofgold.com.

Mel_H: You're the best, sweetie!

Kiyoko_K: I haven't even TOLD U
the best yet! Missy and Veronica
are coming here right after their
shift is done at Macy's. They're
dying to see the famous Hudson-
Bennett caf so I told them you
could do your interview there!

Mel_H: At this rate, I'm gonna
have everything I need for this
article by the end of the day!!!

Kiyoko_K: Well, you better! Tomorrow
you have to write the thing and
tomorrow night, we're doing our photo
shoot in Emma's studio. (Ooh, btw,
did I tell you I called Emma and
asked her if we could use her studio
for our shoot? Of course she said
yes. Emma's my yoga goddess hero.)

Mel_H: And on Friday, we rest.

Kiyoko_K: Are you kidding?
Maybe you've forgotten that
we still have six weeks left
in this crazy internship?

Mel_H: Well, if this article
pans out, I do.

Kiyoko_K: Hey, none of that
now. You're gonna blow Bishop
away and U know it.

       ⓖ   ⓖ   ⓖ   ⓖ

The next night, Mel showed up at Emma's studio bleary-eyed after a long day of writing. She was clutching the printout of her article in her hand like a talisman.

Actually, it was the third draft of the article. She'd written the first draft the night before, staying up till the wee hours in one of the loft's cushiest chairs, typing away on her laptop (and feeling grateful that her path never crossed with Nick's that evening).

She'd written the second draft early that morning, when the *Flirt* cube farm was still largely empty.

Finally, she'd swallowed hard and tiptoed down the row of editors' offices until she reached the one whose plaque read *Quinn Carson—Managing Editor*.

She knocked on Quinn's door, biting her lip and almost hoping he wasn't in. She'd skillfully managed to avoid Quinn ever since their completely embarrassing plane trip.

But now, something bigger than Mel's pride was at stake. So when Quinn called out, "Come in!" Mel squared her shoulders, pasted on a smile, and plunged through the door.

"Well, hello!" Quinn said, grinning at Mel from behind his huge desk. "What a surprise. I was beginning to think that your entire internship would pass without us exchanging a word. *Another* word, that is. I do recall having a fascinating conversation with you recently in first class."

"Ugh," Mel said, rolling her eyes. "I acted like such a dork on that trip. I want to apologize for that. Let's just say I've learned a lot since then."

"Oh?" Quinn said. He sat back in his leather chair and motioned Mel to one of the cowhide chairs in front of his desk.

"What is it with all the furry cow chairs?" Mel muttered as she sat down.

"See, that's the Mel I met," Quinn said. "Never

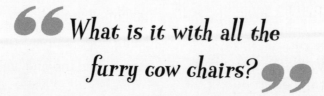

What is it with all the furry cow chairs?

afraid to speak her mind."

"Well, I've been doing that a lot lately," Mel said. "And maybe not always the right way. But now I've written something that I think is good. It's very *Flirt*."

"And that's a good thing?" Quinn said. "What about *The New Yorker*? What about covering the women's movement in Afghanistan?"

"Oh, I still want those things," Mel said quickly. "But *Flirt*? Well, let's just say that it's no stepping stone. I'd be proud to have an article in this mag. If it's good enough, that is. That's why I'm here. I wrote this article that's due to Ms. Bishop tomorrow."

"Ooh," Quinn cringed. "She's a tough editor."

"I know," Mel said. "I've written two drafts already, and now I was wondering if you could take a look at it. Maybe give me some pointers for my third draft?"

Quinn grinned and extended a hand.

"Hand it over," he said of Mel's printout. "I'll give it a look and have it back to you, full of red ink, no doubt, in about an hour."

"Thanks, Quinn!" Mel exclaimed, jumping to her feet and heading for the door. "I really appreciate it."

"You should," Quinn joked. "I'm a tough editor, but compared to Josephine Bishop I'm a big softie. The hard part's yet to come."

After Mel had gotten Quinn's comments on her article (and there had been quite a lot of them), she'd spent the afternoon slaving away on her final draft.

Around five o'clock, she finally felt like she'd gotten it right. It was twelve hundred words of perfection.

Which meant it was time to get ready for her close-up!

ⓖ　　ⓖ　　ⓖ　　ⓖ

Kiyoko, Mel, and Olivia were prepped for the photo shoot by seven P.M. Sha-Say—his hair pulled into two fizzy pigtails and dressed from head to toe in skintight, purple leather—had coated each of the girls' faces with a rainbow of colors mixed from Minnie's fabulous spectrum of makeup.

Meanwhile, Charlotte had pitched in on the hairdos.

Mel hadn't expected to see Charlotte that evening. After all, whither Genevieve went, Charlotte always seemed to follow. But soon after Mel arrived at the studio, Charlotte showed up at the door, looking sheepish.

"Um, listen you guys," she said. "I know something's going on here because Genevieve's been in a snit about it all day. In fact, she's in such a snit that she just blew me off to go get a mani-pedi at Bliss spa. Apparently, they only had one appointment available."

Charlotte rolled her eyes and gave a dubious snort. Mel couldn't help laughing out loud.

"So, I was just wondering," Charlotte said, "what *are* you up to?"

"It's a photo shoot," Alexa admitted. "For Mel's story. Genevieve wasn't exactly included."

"But Charlotte," Mel said immediately, "you're welcome to stay. In fact, we could probably use another model. We're doing a photo shoot for my DIY-makeup story. Faces only. Want in?"

"Oh, no!" Charlotte said, waving Mel off. "Modeling's not my thing. Unless you have some kickin' athletic gear and you need some action shots. But did you know I'm also a whiz with a blow-dryer?"

"Hey, girl," Kiyoko said, taking her hair out of the bun on top of her head so it cascaded down her back, "have at the locks. And give me something creative!"

Mel had to giggle as out-there Sha-Say and prim little Charlotte worked side by side, making up the "models."

And she *really* laughed when their work was done. She couldn't stop staring at her reflection in the mirror. Her eyes had been painted with about half a dozen clashing colors, yet they didn't look weird or garish. In fact, they looked as huge as saucers and more blue than they'd ever looked before. Her lips were wild, too. From one angle, they looked pink; from another, lilac; and from a third, brown. They looked like an exotic flower. Finally, Mel's hair was pulled into a floppy bow on top of her head.

Kiyoko and Olivia looked equally exotic. White stripes emanated from Kiyoko's almond eyes and her lips were glossed with sheer iridescence. Her hair had been frizzed around her face in a wild halo. Meanwhile, Olivia's skin had been enhanced by an array of creamy peaches and pinks, and false eyelashes made her eyes look dewy and gorgeous.

"Okay, you guys," Alexa finally announced, picking up her camera. "I was going to shoot each of you separately, but I've decided to go a different way. Put those faces together and vamp for me, girls. This is gonna be a group shoot!"

Mel giggled as Kiyoko and Olivia crowded their pretty faces up against hers and Alexa began clicking away.

Mel didn't know if she'd lived up to Bishop's standards with her article and, now, this photo shoot.

But she did know she'd given it a *Flirt*-worthy shot.

ⓒ　　ⓒ　　ⓒ　　ⓒ

The next morning Mel beat Bishop to the office. She decided to wait for the editor in Delia's anteroom. She smoothed her sleek powder blue skirt and cream-colored sweater before sitting down. In her lap, she held a laser-printed copy of her article and the contact sheets from Alexa's photo shoot.

After an excruciating twenty-minute wait, Bishop strode into the office, a cardboard cup of tea in one hand, her briefcase in the other.

Mel stood up and smiled at her.

"I have the story ready," she announced. "First thing Friday morning, just as you asked."

Bishop raised her eyebrows. Then she checked out Mel's outfit. Finally, she allowed a hint of a smile to cross her lips.

"Good, Melanie," she said briskly. "Leave it on Delia's desk, please. I'll look at it shortly and let you know my response."

Mel walked out of the office on shaky legs.

Then she sleepwalked through much of the day as she waited for a word from Bishop.

It didn't come until four o'clock. By then, many of the Flirters in the cube farm were beginning to wrap up their work to take off early for the weekend.

All bustling stopped, however, when Josephine Bishop strode across the room. Because Josephine Bishop almost *never* entered the cube farm.

She proceeded all the way to the wall and stopped in front of Mel's desk.

"Melanie," she said.

"Ms. Bishop!" Mel replied, jumping to her feet. Bishop was holding Mel's article in her hand. Even

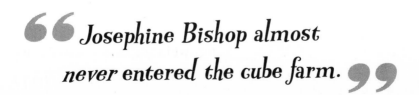

Josephine Bishop almost never entered the cube farm.

through the back of the pages, Mel could see that the text was littered with red markings.

Her heart sank.

I can't believe it, she thought, trying to keep her face from crumpling in disappointment. *All that work and she still didn't like it.*

"I gave your article a fair amount of line editing," Bishop announced. "It's a little rough around the edges. But in terms of content? Of voice and tone? Of its *Flirt* factor? It's very good, Melanie. Very good indeed."

"Really?" Mel squealed, jumping up and down. It took several seconds for her to remember that Bishop was not a jumping-up-and-down kind of lady. Mel stopped abruptly and tried to keep from grinning too hard.

"I want you to take a crack at my edits," Bishop said, handing the article to Mel. "You can have Monday to work on it, but have it in to me first thing Tuesday morning."

> **Maybe Alexa is ready for more than product shots.**

"Yes, ma'am," Mel agreed happily.

"Oh, and Melanie," Bishop added. "The photographs are excellent, as well. I think I detect the work of Sha-Say?"

"And the work of Alexa Veron," Mel said proudly. Nearby, she could see Alexa pumping her fist in the air and smiling like mad.

"Yes, well maybe Alexa is ready for more than product shots," Bishop confirmed. "But we'll see."

With that, Bishop walked serenely back toward her office.

Which meant Kiyoko, Alexa, Olivia, Mel, and Charlotte were free to form a tight little circle and cackle at their victory. They hopped around, rubbed their hands together, and giggled wildly.

Only Genevieve, sitting silently at her desk, didn't join in the fun. She merely shot Mel a sullen look, then stalked away.

Mel couldn't even bring herself to be too distressed over Genevieve's pique. After two weeks fraught with mistakes, she'd finally done something right.

And she intended to celebrate.

ⓖ　　　ⓖ　　　ⓖ　　　ⓖ

That night, Mel didn't have to elbow her way into the bathroom to get herself glammed up. She was the guest of honor there. As she whisked on blush, mascara, and a creative mix of lipsticks, she and her friends dished about Bishop's incredible reaction to Mel's story—and about the effort they'd all put into it.

"We deserve a night on the town!" Kiyoko shouted, setting all the girls laughing.

All of them, once again, except Genevieve, who was sulking in her bedroom. Her absence was a bit glaring, especially to Charlotte.

"I don't know what to do," she whispered to Mel. "I want to go out with you guys tonight. But Genevieve is my oldest friend. Maybe I should stay here with her."

"That does it," Mel said. She marched to the bedroom and stalked through the door.

"Put on something fun," she ordered her roommate. Even as she said it, she had reservations. Genevieve's expression was more sour than ever. "We're going out."

"You don't want me along," Genevieve sniped from her bed. "If you did, you might have invited me to your little fashion shoot."

"It wasn't little," Mel said frankly. "It was fabulous. That's because my friends helped me out with it. That's what friends do. Maybe you could take a lesson from them, Genevieve."

"I don't know what you're talking about," Genevieve grumbled.

"You know exactly what I'm talking about," Mel insisted. "You've pretended to be nice to me, but you haven't really been nice at all. *But*, we're roommates. We're fellow interns. We're all in this together. Which means you have to come out with us tonight. Just like Bishop, I give people second chances."

"Really?" Genevieve quavered, swinging her legs off the bed. "Well, where are we going?"

"I don't know!" Mel said happily. "We'll decide on

the fly. There's a whole city out there for us to explore and I can't wait!"

⟡   ⟡   ⟡   ⟡

Within ten minutes the six girls were ready, dressed in an assortment of swingy skirts, skinny jeans, sparkly tops, and strappy shoes. They started laughing and having fun before they even summoned the elevator.

When the elevator arrived, the door *clunked* open to reveal Nick, wearing his waiter clothes and carrying a bag of art supplies. When he saw Mel, his face went pink. Mel felt her cheeks flush as well.

"Uh, hi," Nick said hesitantly.

An awkward pause filled the room. Around her, Mel's friends shuffled their feet uncomfortably. Mel had to fill the silence.

"So, how'd the show go the other night?" she asked. "Did you sell any paintings?"

"Yeah, I did, actually," Nick said. "Two of them. Thanks for asking."

"Well, it was a really cool show," Mel said. Then she grinned. "I mean, *I* didn't exactly have a great time, what

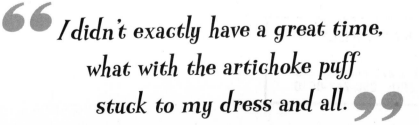

I didn't exactly have a great time, what with the artichoke puff stuck to my dress and all.

with the artichoke puff stuck to my dress and all . . ."

Nick laughed.

So Nick has a girlfriend, Mel thought with relief. *That doesn't mean he's not a nice guy. Why shouldn't we keep on being friends?*

And besides, she added with a gleam in her eyes, *Anastasia seems like the fickle type. You never know what could happen to that relationship over the next six weeks.*

Mel waved good-bye to Nick, beckoned to her buds, and stepped into the elevator.

Soon the interns were stalking together down the sidewalks of SoHo, their arms linked and their hair blowing in the warm, almost-July breezes. They were intent on soaking in all the excitement of New York City on a Friday night.

For the first time since arriving in the city, Mel felt like a native. Very adventurous. Very confident.

And very *Flirty*.